THE EBOLA CONNECTION

A Novel

Paul D. Ellner

For Toby,
With gratitude and
warm regards

Paul

4/2/18

ISBN: 978-1-63492-176-3

Published by BookLocker.com, Inc., St. Petersburg, Florida.

Printed on acid-free paper.

BookLocker.com, Inc.
2017

First Edition

For David and Jonathan

In the year 1976, evil emerged from the African jungle as a deadly disease. After killing many people, it disappeared only to reappear many miles away. Like a panther, the disease crouched in the bush knowing that the time to pounce again would come.

1

Hartford, Connecticut, Saturday May 20, 2006 6 p.m.

Howard Frazer snapped the textbook shut with a sense of finality and slid it into his backpack. *I hope this is the last time I'll have to deal with French irregular verbs.*

His brother Frank entered the room they shared and flung himself onto his bed.

"Tennis is a quaint sport," he said. Frank had been watching a tennis match on the TV.

"Quaint?" Howard said.

Frank's vocabulary was considerably more advanced than that of a typical 15-year old.

"What do you mean?" Howard said.

"Well, for one thing, they keep score by fives. Instead of one, two, three, it's five, fifteen, thirty, and so on. And for nothing, they say 'love'. It doesn't make sense."

"Why does that bother you?" Howard asked.

"I don't know. Why couldn't they say, 'zero' or 'zip'?" Frank said.

Howard laughed, shrugged, and regarded the tuxedo laid out on his bed. *It looks something like a uniform. Well, in a way it is the uniform of people who have succeeded. For me, I succeeded in graduating high school. I would like to succeed . . .at something more.*

Frank had accompanied Howard to the rental store.

"I like the colored ones," Frank volunteered. "I'd get one of those."

Howard shook his head. "I'll stick to the regular black."

Howard also rented a pair of shiny leather shoes.At home, he told his brother, "I'm going to shower," and hurried down the hall to the bathroom. As he stood under the warm spray, he thought, *finally, the Senior Prom and a date with Cathy*. Although thoughts of Cathy always produced a stirring in his loins, Howard considered the Senior Prom to be more important than a date with Cathy. The prom symbolized the end of high school for him and the beginning of real life.

He knew there was no money for college. *I don't care, I'm not sure I'm bright enough, but maybe Frank will be able to wangle a scholarship.*

Back in the room, he toweled himself dry. Frank had gone back to the living room and the tennis match. Howard found clean underwear in a drawer and dressed in the tuxedo. He tied the laces on the black shoes, looked in the small mirror on top of the dresser, and combed his straw-colored hair. It took him three times to get the part right. Finally, he clipped the bow tie to his collar and satisfied with its appearance, stopped at his mother's room where there was a full-length mirror on the back of the door. He glanced at his reflection and smiled. *Cathy will be blown away when she sees me.*

He bounded down the stairs to the kitchen. His mother was at the sink chopping vegetables for tomorrow's beef stew.

"How do I look, Ma?" he asked.

Clara studied her son. "Very handsome," she said with a smile. She dried her hands on a dishtowel, adjusted his bow tie, which was askew, and kissed him on the cheek. She could detect stubble, not yet visible, but refrained from making a comment. *No girl would consider Howard handsome.* She knew her seventeen-year old son's muscular, 5′ 8″ frame could be considered formidable, but those clear brown eyes peering from an open and friendly face would belie that impression.

"Don't forget Cathy's corsage," she said.

"Thanks, Ma," he told her. He kissed her, collected the flowers from the refrigerator, and started for the door.

"Have a good time at the prom. Drive carefully," she called after him.

Clara watched her son leave. *I wish I could hug him, but he wouldn't like that. He looks so much like his father. Michael would have been proud that Howard finished high school. Michael was a good man, a good husband, and a hard worker. He always brought his wages home, never showed up drunk, gambled, or played around. He was happy when Howard was born and overjoyed when Frank came along. It was only a few weeks later after Frank was born when my poor Michael fell off that high girder. Both boys knew the story of their father's fatal accident. His safety harness didn't work. The damn lock failed. The $750,000 from the company's and Michael's life insurance sounded like a lot at the time, but over the years, it barely covered raising the two boys. Howard tried to help part-time after school. He started working in the hardware store when he was 16. Frank was too young to work. I wish Michael could be sitting with me at the graduation ceremony.* Clara sighed and went back to chopping vegetables.

Replete in his rented tuxedo with corsage in hand, Howard's excitement grew anticipating the prom and his date with Cathy. He started out in the family's 2001 Toyota, and after thirty minutes pulled up in front of Cathy's apartment house. She lived in a section somewhat more upscale than his. It occurred to him he had never been inside her apartment nor had he met her parents. *Maybe they don't like her going out with me. Maybe they think I'm not good enough for her.* He blew the horn once. *I remember when I brought her home. Mom liked her. She said she seemed like a nice girl. She is a nice girl. Frank thought she was pretty.*

Howard recalled how they met six months ago. *Cathy, 16 and a junior, was strolling down a corridor with a group of girls, chatting with them, oblivious to all else. The corridor was lined with student lockers, one of which had an open door. I saw she was heading for a collision, took her elbow, and steered her clear of the obstruction. She looked surprised, and her girlfriends giggled. She thanked me and asked my name.*

This encounter led to a date. They had a good time and began to see each other regularly. He was dependable, and she felt safe when she was with him. Cathy liked him. For his part, Howard liked dating an attractive girl who was bright and popular.

Cathy came out and walked to the car. She wore a lavender knee-length prom dress. Howard got out and held the door open for her. He felt awkward and self-conscious in the tuxedo and stiff shoes.

"You look beautiful," he said. He could not help noticing the strapless top revealing the cleavage of her young breasts.

"Thank you," she said. "You look great."

When they were both inside the car he handed her the wrist corsage.

"Oh, it's gorgeous," she said and slipped it on her wrist.

They drove to the banquet hall, listening to popular songs on the radio. Students began to arrive, mostly in small groups. Howard and Cathy joined other couples walking into the hall. Cathy seemed slightly nervous. "This is the first Senior Prom I've ever been to," she confided.

"It's my first one, too. Don't worry, we'll be fine," he reassured her. Inside, they heard music provided by a disc jockey.

"Let's get our picture taken," Cathy said, and they joined a queue of other couples waiting to be photographed. When it came their turn, they posed side by side.

"Say cheese," the photographer urged, and both managed to smile.

They found a table and sat down. A waiter appeared and asked, "Which meal did you select?"

"I'll have the chicken," Howard said.

"Same here," Cathy said.

"And to drink?" the waiter asked.

"Pepsi," they chorused.

"Do you want to dance?" Cathy asked.

"I don't know how to dance," Howard said.

"It's easy. I'll show you. C'mon."

She took his hand and pulled him. Howard reluctantly stood up and followed her to the crowded dance floor. He tried to follow her by mimicking the same contortions of others around him.

"I really don't know what the hell I'm doing," he said.

Cathy grinned at him, "You're doing great."

Howard thought the music would never end so they could sit. He saw the waiter delivering their drinks, and he used this as an excuse to return to the table. They sat, each having nothing to say, watching the dancers. "C'mon, let's dance," Cathy urged, dragging Howard back to the dance floor. After a time, he relaxed and started to enjoy it.

"Are you having fun?" she asked.

"Yeah, it's cool."

When the music stopped, the D.J. announced, "I'm going to take a break so you can all enjoy your dinner. Don't forget to vote for your king and queen of the prom."

After Howard and Cathy finished eating, she said, "Let's go vote." They voted and returned to find dessert waiting, a marbled cake with ice cream along side.

"That was yummy," Cathy said. "Let's dance."

Eventually, the D.J. played a slow dance, and Howard took Cathy in his arms. He did not know any steps, but he held her close, and they swayed to the music. Howard was stirred by the fragrance she wore. When the song ended, Howard asked, "What do you say we leave now?"

"But we won't find out who got to be king and queen," Cathy said.

"I don't care who they are," Howard said. "Do you?"

"Not really. Let's go. Let's find a place where we can be alone."

Howard was encouraged. He felt she was looking forward to a session of lovemaking. He drove to the boat ramp parking lot near the Connecticut River and parked facing the water. It was the darkest and most inconspicuous location he could find. For a while, they sat listening to the radio play current songs and watching the lights on the water. He turned the engine off but kept the radio playing.

"How did you like the prom?" he asked.

"It was a lovely evening, and now we can have some private time together." She turned and gave him a lingering kiss.

"Would you like some vodka?" Howard asked displaying a small bottle purchased for him by an older friend. He unscrewed the top and offered it to Cathy.

"I don't want any," she said. "I don't like that stuff."

"Yeah, it's too strong." He closed the bottle and put it away. "I have a joint we could share," Howard offered, producing a marijuana cigarette.

"O.K.," she said.

He lit the joint and took a drag before passing it to her. "Don't wet it," he cautioned.

She took it from him and inhaled some of the smoke. Cathy had done this on other occasions. They continued to share the joint until it was consumed. He tossed the stub out the window, looking around to make certain they were alone.

"Come closer," he said.

Howard put his arm around Cathy, drew her to him, and kissed her. Her tongue darted into his mouth. They continued kissing, each kiss becoming more heated. As she expected, Howard tried to fondle her breast, but the thick material of the dress interfered. Cathy unzipped the bodice freeing her breast. He bent and kissed it, taking her nipple into his mouth. He felt her shudder as it hardened. They were both aroused. Cathy reached over and felt his hardness trying to escape. She unzipped his fly, freeing his erection. She bent down to take him between her lips. Cathy knew

Howard liked it. They had done this before. Her best friend, Selma, had told her about oral sex. "It's called a blow job. You can't get pregnant or catch a disease. A lot of the girls do it."

After a few minutes, Howard finished with a sharp intake of breath, an orgasmic "Aahh", and smiled. Cathy handed him a tissue she had ready. They continued to fondle each other. Howard moved his hand up her thigh and felt the moist heat between her legs.

"Let's do it," Howard whispered. "I really want to."

"I do, too, but I don't want to get pregnant."

"Aren't you on the pill?"

"No, my father wouldn't permit it," she lied. She would not dare bring up the subject of birth control with either of her parents.

"I've got a condom," he told her. Like many other high school boys, Howard kept a condom in his wallet in the hope someday he would have the opportunity to use it.

A year ago, Cathy had sexual intercourse several times with a former boyfriend, and she liked it. Now she wanted to do it with Howard.

"O.K.," she said, "but let's get in the back seat." Other than the oral sex with Cathy, this would be Howard's first sexual experience involving someone other than himself.

Afterwards, he helped her to zip up her dress, and he rearranged his clothing.

Cathy asked, "What time is it? I've got to be home before midnight."

"Or else you'll turn into a pumpkin," Howard joked, now more confidant.

"More likely pumpkin pie," Cathy said thinking of how irate her father could get.

He started the engine and drove away. In front of her house, he got out to open the door for her.

"That was awesome," Howard whispered, thinking of the sex.

"Goodnight, Howard," she said and kissed him, glancing to see if anyone was watching. "I had a lovely time."

Early the next morning Howard pulled on jeans and a sweatshirt, tiptoed downstairs and outside to sit on the front steps. The neighborhood was in an older section of Hartford, along Blue Hills Avenue. The street was quiet, not many people moving about on a Sunday morning.

Howard thought about the previous evening. His thoughts turned to Cathy, and he smiled. *I did it—we did it. It felt good—I think she liked it, too. I feel like a real man—we can do it again if she wants now that I've crossed that bridge.*

Frank came downstairs and sat next to his brother. "How was the prom?" Frank asked.

"It was O.K."

"What did you and Cathy do afterward?"

"Nothing much. We just drove around for a while, and then I took her home," Howard said. He knew Frank wanted to ask if they had sex. But he was not about to tell him.

Frank looked at him knowingly and smiled.

2

Friday, June 16

Clara Frazer put on her best dress for Howard's graduation.

"It pisses me off to have to pay for the cap and gown," Howard remarked. *Why should I have to pay for an outfit for graduation? The school should supply them.*

Howard drove Clara and Frank to the high school. They were able to get seats near the aisle so Howard would pass close to them as he marched to Elgar's *Pomp and Circumstance* toward his place with the other graduates. Howard's name was not among those receiving various prizes and awards. He had been an average student, collecting mostly B's with only occasional A's and C's.

Clara and Frank cheered when Howard's name was announced as he crossed the stage to receive his diploma. The applause for him was modest compared to the response accorded more popular students. Clara beamed with pride. *If only Michael could see him now.* Rather than participating in extracurricular activities, such as clubs or sports, Howard had elected to work at a part-time job to help the family finances.

When the ceremony was over, Howard drove his family home stopping only to return his cap and gown. In their backyard, the boys lit the charcoal in their small Hibachi, and Clara grilled hot dogs and hamburgers for them. They drank lemonade and ate slices of the chocolate cake she baked for this special occasion.

While Clara busied herself cleaning up, Howard and Frank sat watching the coals of the grill die from embers to ashes.

"So what will you do now?" Frank asked.

"I'm trying to figure out where I go from here," Howard said. "I'd like to be someone important. Someone who helps people, like a lawyer or a doctor, but that takes college. We don't have any money for college."

"I'm going to go to college," Frank said.

"How will you manage that?"

"I'm going to try to get a scholarship to some college. My grades are pretty good," he added, leaving Howard to reflect on his own mediocre academic performance.

"Right now, I think my best bet is to learn a trade so I can make a decent living," Howard said.

"What trade interests you?"

"Maybe a mechanic, an electrician, or a plumber—something like that. A service people will always need regardless of what it costs."

"I suppose that's a good idea," Frank told him without much enthusiasm.

Clara looked out the kitchen window where her sons sat talking. She reflected on the graduation ceremony. *Howard was only three when Michael died. He never had any time with his father. When I graduated, my father wasn't there either, but at least I had the benefit of knowing him. I remember when I was a young girl, not yet in high school, he used to explain science to me. He used to tell me about those Ebola outbreaks in Africa. A terrible disease. I wonder if they have found a cure yet. I hope to God that disease stays in Africa so that my sons or other Americans can never get it.*

3

Friday, June 16, 2006

Howard spent a lot of time thinking about his future. In America, employment growth and economic opportunity had slowed. Jobs were getting hard to find, and some people were being laid off. American troops were still deployed in Iraq.

I've been working part time at the hardware store since I was sixteen—a few hours after school each day and eight hours on Saturday just for minimum wage. Now I need a full time job with better pay.

Howard called shop after shop trying to persuade the tradesman to take him on as an apprentice. He called on mechanics, electricians, and plumbers. After a month of negative results, he finally connected with a small plumbing business. Steven Malloy was the sole plumber and proprietor.

"You're my last stop, Mr. Malloy," Howard told him. "I've tried every place in Hartford looking for a job."

"Call me Steve," Malloy said. "What's your education?"

"I just graduated high school, and I want to learn a trade."

"Well, you've come to the right place. It just so happens I'm looking for a helper. I'll take you on."

Howard's face brightened. "That's great! Thank you."

Steve continued, "The hours are 8-4 weekdays and half a day on Saturday. I'll pay you minimum to start. Get here Monday morning." Howard calculated his salary would be $16,640 a year. He was enthusiastic about his new job and lost no time in sharing the news with his mother.

"I knew you would find something," his mother said. "You were trying so hard. This could be a real opportunity for you to learn the trade."

"Way to go, big brother. A full time job," Frank said. "How much will you make?"

When Howard told him what his wages would be, Frank said, "I guess that's O.K. You'll probably get raises."

Cathy, starting her senior year in high school, was less enthusiastic. It would not be terrific telling her friends that her boyfriend was learning to be a plumber.

"You're going to have to work with all that gook and grime?" she said.

"It's honest work," Howard said. "And plumbers make good money."

Howard showed up Monday morning at the plumber's shop. He wore slacks, a shirt and tie. Steve looked at him disapprovingly and laughed.

"You're going to get those fancy clothes dirty," he told Howard. "Better get some work clothes. Go in the back and find a company shirt to wear."

Howard put the company shirt on over his shirt and tie. *This was not a great start*. He stood around for half an hour not knowing what to do.

Eventually, Steve looked at him and said, "Grab these tools." Howard picked up a heavy bucket containing a collection of wrenches, pliers, screwdrivers, and other tools he could not identify. He accompanied Steve and climbed into a pickup truck.

After twenty minutes of driving in silence, they stopped in front of an old house.

"Grab the tools and come along," Steve said.

Howard followed him inside the house where an aggravated woman greeted them.

"Thank God you came," she said. The woman led them to a bathroom where water had overflowed from the sink.

"This ain't the first time it's happened," she said.

Steve ignored her and got down to look under the sink.

"Got a pail or bucket?" Steve asked while examining the drainpipe. The woman left and returned with a mop bucket, which he put underneath the drainpipe.

"Hand me a pipe wrench," Steve said. Howard looked at the various wrenches in the bucket and was not sure which one the boss wanted. He selected a wrench, hoping it was the correct one and handed it to the boss. Steve shook his head. "Not that one," he growled. "The big one." Howard handed him the biggest wrench.

In a few minutes Steve was able to remove the u-shaped trap and water poured out into the bucket, emptying the sink. He examined the drainpipe. He handed it to Howard.

"Clean it out," Steve told him.

Howard inspected the drain. It appeared to be filled with a large amount of slimy material, hair, buttons, and an earring all among the muck. He did not know how to clean it. He selected a tool with a large brush and asked the woman, "Do you have some newspaper?"

The woman returned with some newspaper, which Howard spread on the floor and using the brush, managed to empty the drainpipe, which he handed back to Steve. He watched as Steve reattached the drain, then stood and opened a faucet. Water flowed into the sink, which started to fill again. Steve turned off the faucet and told Howard, "Get me a snake. It's in the back of the truck."

Howard ran out and found the large coiled metal tool, which he brought back to Steve. Steve threaded the snake down the pipe until it reached the obstruction. He turned the tool a few times until he cleared it.

"That should do it," he told the woman. He secured the drainpipe, tightening it with the wrench.

The woman looked relieved. "How much do I owe you?" she asked.

Steve gestured to Howard. "Clean the place up." He turned to the woman, "I have to go out to the truck to write up the bill. I'll be right back."

While he was gone Howard found the earring, washed it off, and handed it to the woman. He plunged his hand into the muck again and took out the buttons and other solid pieces, which he discarded. Howard poured the water into the toilet and picked up the newspaper from the floor. He used a piece of it to wipe his hands.

Steve returned and handed the bill to the woman. She looked at it and said, "For this much, I could have had a new sink. Will you take a check?" Steve nodded, and in a few minutes she returned with the check.

"Thank you," Steve said. "Let's go," he said to Howard. In the truck, Steve used his cell phone to call his office and check his messages, one of which directed him to the next job.

En route, Howard asked, "What do I have to do to become a licensed plumber?"

"You're a high school graduate, right?" Howard nodded. "You will need about 2,000 hours in a trade school. You can do this at night if you want. Then you have to work as an apprentice for 6,000 hours. That's about three years. After that, you take an exam and, assuming you pass, you become a licensed plumber, what we call a journeyman."

Howard returned home at the end of the day. He was concerned about his performance. *I don't think I made a great start today. I didn't learn anything, but this was only the first day*. He noticed that his fingernails contained black grime, which he tried to clean by vigorous brushing with only partial success. Howard was patient by nature. His temper flared however, when he felt someone took unfair advantage of him. He was also determined. *I know I'll be able to learn this stuff. I'm sure I'll be better tomorrow.*

In the days and weeks that followed, Howard experienced a wide variety of jobs including the installation of a water heater, repair of a garbage disposal unit, broken water lines and stopped up toilets. He felt he was not learning much and planned to register at a trade school in the fall. He was worried that his salary did not contribute enough to the household expenses.

Howard returned home from work one evening, washed up, and joined Frank and his mother at the dinner table. After dinner, he told Clara, "I have to go out and get some information about starting classes at that trade school. I'll be a little late."

Frank joined his brother at the kitchen sink where he washed dishes. "You can dry," Howard said. Frank dried a few dishes, but then said, "Got homework," and left to go upstairs. Howard put the remaining washed dishes in the drainer and left the house. He drove to the Hartford Industrial Trade School that Steve recommended and found a parking place a few blocks away. The admissions office was crowded, and Howard had to wait a long time until he spoke to a staff person. It was after nine o'clock when he finished, and he hurried down the dark street to his car. It was cold, and Howard drew his light jacket around him. The street was empty and not well lit. As Howard walked along he thought he heard a faint cry of "Help". In a few more steps he perceived two men struggling. One man lay on the sidewalk, propped against a building. His hat was off, disclosing a head of scant grey hair. A long white cane lay nearby. The other man punched and kicked him. Howard ran up and yelled, "Leave him alone!" The attacker looked over his shoulder at Howard and growled, "Fuck off!" He turned his attention to his victim and demanded, "Gimmie your wallet!" He punched his victim again.

Howard grabbed the attacker and threw him to the ground. The assailant reached into his pocket as if to retrieve a weapon. Howard punched the man in the stomach and sat on his chest.

"Get offa me, you asshole . . . cocksucker . . . motherfucker," he gasped. This last expletive enraged Howard who punched him in the face causing blood to flow from his nose.

The victim called to Howard, "I got a cell phone—I called 911."

The attacker, snorting blood, managed to say, "Lemme go. You can keep the wallet."

Howard wiped the blood from his hands on the man's jacket, but continued to hold him on the ground.

In a few minutes, a police car arrived, blue lights flashing. Two officers jumped from the car. One of them went over to the victim, while the other officer went over to Howard who climbed off the attacker.

"This guy was robbing that man . . . punching him. I think maybe he's blind," Howard said, recognizing the long cane.

"Yeah," the officer said and turned to the assailant. "Get up! Hands behind your back."

The attacker stood sullenly silent as the officer handcuffed and thrust him into the rear of the patrol car.

An ambulance arrived. Two Emergency Technicians emerged with a stretcher and placed the injured man on it.

"My hat, my cane," the man called. "Thank you, young man," he called to Howard as they lifted him into the ambulance.

A few people leaving the school hurried away from the scene.

One of the officers asked Howard his name. He produced his driving license.

"What were you doing here?" the officer asked. Howard explained he had just left school when he heard and saw the assault.

"Are you O.K.?" the officer asked him.

"Yeah. I'm parked just down the block," he told the officer. "I'm heading home."

"We might need you to come down to the station as a witness," the officer said.

As he drove home, Howard felt he had done something good. It was eleven o'clock when he reached his house. His mother had gone to bed, but Frank woke when Howard entered their room to undress.

"What happened to your knee?" Frank asked.

Howard saw that his knee was scraped and bloody.

"I fell and scraped it," he told his brother, who went back to sleep.

Howard washed his knee with soap and water and went to bed.

The next evening, while the family ate dinner, the doorbell rang. Howard admitted a man who identified himself as a reporter from the *Hartford Courant,* a local newspaper.

"Are you Howard Frazer?" he asked.

"Yes, what can I do for you?"

"I'd like to ask you a few questions about what happened last night," the reporter said.

"Well we're eating dinner. I'll try to answer your questions," Howard said.

As requested Howard described the incident. "I found this guy beating up and trying to rob a blind old man. While I pulled the attacker off him, the man called 911 with his cell. The police came and arrested the attacker."

"Was there a fight?" the reporter asked.

"Yeah, I had to knock him down and sit on him until the cops came."

Clara and Frank sat in stunned silence.

"The man you saved was eighty-four and blind. His name is Charles Becker. He had a couple of broken ribs, but he's going to be O.K."

After a few more questions, the reporter thanked Howard.

"We need more people like you who won't tolerate crime," he said getting up to leave.

"Will this be in the newspaper?" Frank asked.

"It could be," the reporter said and left.

Howard thought about his job. *I've been working for Steve for six months now. I think I've done a good job.* He approached Steve on a Saturday afternoon, just before quitting time.

"Steve, I been working for you for six months. Are you satisfied with my performance?"

"You've been doing O.K.," Steve said.

"In that case, do you think you could give me a raise, since I'm only getting the minimum wage?"

Steve shook his head. "First of all, you're still an apprentice and have a lot to learn. It's too soon. Maybe in the future."

Howard became discouraged.

4

Frank was in his junior year in high school. He was already as tall as Howard with a slimmer build. Any girl would consider him good looking. He got good grades, worked on the school paper, and was popular with his classmates. He made the track team, running the quarter-mile dash. Frank liked to win regardless of how he did it. He and Howard had always been close. In grade school, Howard protected Frank from being bullied by a group of older boys. When Howard appeared on the scene, the bullies decided to leave the Frazer brothers alone.

When the boys played cards together, Howard sometimes saw that Frank cheated.

"Oh, I'm sorry. I made a mistake," Frank said.

But when this happened several times, Howard told him, "Look Frank, you're cheating. If I catch you cheating again, I won't play cards with you anymore."

"O.K., O.K.," Frank said. "I won't do it again."

While this put an end to the cheating incidents, there were other times when Howard had to question his brother's honesty. On one such occasion, Howard watched Frank and his friends play catch with a baseball. The boys were wearing mitts and competing to see who could throw the ball harder. Finally, Frank threw the ball as hard as he could. It was a wild throw that sailed over the catcher's head to break a window in an adjoining apartment. The owner, an elderly man, looked out from the broken pane and demanded, "Who did that?"

"It was Jerry," Frank yelled, pointing to the catcher.

"No, it wasn't me, it was him," the boy shouted indicating Frank.

"I'm going to call the police!" the man threatened.

Howard saw the entire incident and called Frank over to him.

"Why did you lie? I saw what happened. I saw you break the window. If you don't tell that man it was you who broke his window, I'll tell Mom and the police."

Frank became frightened. "I'll have to pay for it," he cried. "How can I do that?"

"I'll help you," Howard said. "And Mom won't know about it. Now go over, tell the man you did it, and we'll pay for the damage. Then tell Jerry you're sorry you tried to blame him."

Frank was well aware of his status as Clara's favorite, and he was concerned a report of this mischief could let Howard usurp his position.

"O.K., O.K.," Frank said and confessed his misdeed to the man and to Jerry.

Frank joined the tennis club and learned the game. He spent a lot of time writing applications for college admission.

"How do you expect to pay for college?" Howard asked him.

"I'm hoping to get a scholarship," Frank said. "And maybe I'll take out a student loan."

Cathy found a job as a waitress in a local restaurant. She continued to date Howard, but was not particularly impressed with his choice of a vocation.

"Plumbing is a filthy blue collar job, mostly involved with cleaning out people's toilets," she said.

"Somebody has to do it," Howard said with a shrug.

Cathy was an only child. Her father, an insurance broker, was a martinet who established rules for all

Cathy's activities. Her mother, a small timid woman, was a mouse who quivered whenever her husband thundered. Her parents did not encourage Cathy to think about college. Cathy spent as much time as she could away from home.

"I don't know exactly what I want to do," she said to Howard one day, "but I don't want to spend my life as a waitress. I am a mediocre student, but there must be something better I can do." She respected Howard for his mature opinions, and they had become friends as well as lovers.

"You need to talk to someone who might be able to help you," Howard said.

"Yeah, but who?"

Howard thought for a moment. "Why don't you talk with my Mom? She's pretty level headed. You could come over for dinner."

On the following Friday evening, Cathy knocked at the door of the Frazer house. Clara opened the door to greet her.

"Hi Cathy, nice to see you again. Come in. Howard is upstairs in the shower. He will be down soon."

"I really appreciate your willingness to talk with me, Mrs. Frazer. I can use some advice."

Clara led Cathy into the kitchen and set a plate of cheese and crackers before her.

"So how can I help you?" Clara asked.

"I just don't want to continue working as a waitress," Cathy said. "I'd like to find something better after high school."

"What do you like to do?" Clara said. "Do you like working with people or with things? It's important to like what you do. For example, I was always interested in science, especially biology, so I became a tech in a microbiology lab. What I suggest is that you checkout a community college and see what kind of programs they offer. You could take evening classes if you need to keep working."

"Thanks so much, Mrs. Frazer," she said and walked into the dining room. Cathy could hear Howard talking to Frank as they came downstairs.

At dinner, Clara continued her conversation with Cathy. "You might try UCONN," she said.

"Do you plan to go to college?" Frank asked.

"Yes, I'm considering that," Cathy said.

"Cool," Frank said.

Throughout dinner, Cathy was aware that Frank had been watching her in a different way. *He's just checking me out. After all, I'm his brother's girlfriend.*

"Do you want to take in a movie?" Howard asked Cathy. "They're playing Harry Potter at the cinema."

"I'd like that. I love those Harry Potter movies, even though they are kind of weird."

Cathy offered to help with the dishes, but Clara shooed both of them out of the kitchen. "Enjoy the movie," she said.

Howard was reading a magazine when an ad encouraging enlistment in the U.S. Army caught his attention. The ad promised a rewarding career as well as the satisfaction of service to the country.

That could be exciting—fighting in battles—but I don't want to kill anybody. He recalled seeing reruns of the *MASH* TV series with Alan Alda as an army doctor and all those army nurses and medical personnel. In addition to the funny repartee, Howard remembered how the medical team helped wounded soldiers. He was impressed by their strong motivation. *I'd like to do that. Help wounded soldiers. I couldn't be a doctor or a nurse, but maybe I could be a medic. A combat medic. I'd like that.*

5

Howard called the recruiting station in Hartford and spoke to the sergeant.

"What's your name?" the sergeant asked.

"Frazer. Howard Frazer."

"What can I do for you, Frazer?" the sergeant said.

"I'm considering enlisting," Howard said. "How much would I make to start?"

"You would start as an E-1, a private. A private makes $18,378 a year. But wait," the sergeant said, mimicking the hucksters of TV and radio, "that's not all. The army will provide you with food, uniforms, healthcare, insurance, and paid vacations. You can make a career in the army, learn a specialty, and serve your country. Is there a particular specialty you might want to learn?" the sergeant asked.

Howard considered the question. *I'd prefer helping people rather than killing them.* "Could I become a medic?"

"That would be as a Health Care Specialist, 68W. If you qualify and complete your specialty training, you would automatically be promoted to E-3, a private first-class with a pay grade of $21,661." Howard was impressed. *It's a hell of a lot more than I'd be making for the rest of my apprenticeship as a plumber.*

"Why don't you come down to the recruiting station and see if you are physically qualified?" the sergeant said.

Howard discussed the idea with his mother.

"What do you think, Mom?"

"I don't like that idea," Clara said. "You could be sent to Iraq and get yourself killed. Hundreds of soldiers come back with that PTSD, whatever that is or minus an arm or a leg."

"But Mom, it's only for four years, and I would be a medic. There's a good chance I would remain here in the U.S." Howard did not use the term "combat medic".

After more discussion, Clara reluctantly agreed. *There is no way I can stop him once he makes up his mind.*

Frank was enthusiastic about the idea of Howard enlisting in the army.

"You will get to see different places," Frank said. "It will be an adventure."

Cathy also thought it was a great idea.

"It's a lot better than being a plumber," she said. "Anyway, it's a lot cleaner."

Neither Frank nor Cathy considered the possible hazards of soldiering.

As directed by the recruiting sergeant, Howard reported to a large medical facility in downtown Hartford. He found about twenty other men all waiting, sitting on benches. About one third of them were African Americans.

A sergeant appeared and announced, "When I call your name, come up and get one of these plastic cups with your name on it. Urinate in the cup in the bathroom, replace the lid, and leave it there. You will be called for an exam which takes about twenty minutes."

The sergeant started to call names. "Jose Ramirez." The man sitting to Howard's right responded, "Aqui—here," and rose to retrieve his cup. The man on

Howard's left remarked, "Damn Spic—can't even speak English."

"Fuck you, asshole," Ramirez retorted.

The man on Howard's left jumped up and started for Ramirez, intending to attack him. Emboldened by his fight with the robber a few months ago, Howard stuck out his leg, tripping the man, and causing him to fall flat on his face. Howard jumped up and sat on his back, pinning him to the floor. The room grew silent as everybody watched. Howard grabbed a handful of the man's hair and moved his head up and down forcing his face to the floor each time.

"I can smash your face down on this tile floor," Howard told him. "That will spoil your good looks and your chance to get into the army. I'm going to do it unless you tell Ramirez you will leave him alone!"

The room remained quiet. A few men applauded, and the sergeant yelled, "Hey, knock it off."

One of the African Americans called out, "They just playing, Sarge."

The man groaned, "O.K., O.K., I'll leave him alone." Howard got off his back, offered a hand to help him up which was shrugged away.

The sergeant resumed calling names. "Leonard Lynch." The man Howard had tripped wiped his face off and went to retrieve his cup. When he returned to his seat, he hissed, "I won't forget this."

"I suggest you don't," Howard said.

"Thanks, man," Ramirez said sliding a wicked-looking switchblade back into his pocket.

Howard trembled. *How did I have the guts to get involved? Other than protecting Frank, I've never been in a fight.*

The sergeant called Howard to get his urine cup.

Howard passed a rigorous physical. Two of the men failed and were sent home. Those remaining were asked to stand. An army officer came out and administered the Oath of Allegiance to the United States.

"You men are now members of the U.S. Army," the officer announced. "Your first order is to go home, pack a small bag, and report here at zero six hundred tomorrow morning. Dismissed!"

Howard went home and told his mother and Frank he had enlisted.

"Where will they send you?" Clara asked.

"I think to Fort Sill for basic training. It's in Oklahoma."

Howard called Steve. "I'm quitting," he said.

"I hope you know what you're doing," Steve said.

"I think I do. Thanks for taking me on when I needed a job."

"You didn't give me any notice," Steve grumbled. "Anyway, good luck."

Howard phoned Cathy to tell her the news.

"I'm in," he said.

She was excited. "That's great. I guess we won't be seeing each other for a while."

"I'm leaving tomorrow morning. I'd like to see you this evening. I'll pick you up at 6. Is that O.K.?"

"That sounds good."

Howard took her to dinner at an Italian bistro. When it was dark, they parked in the usual spot by the river. Later, in front of her house, Howard kissed her goodnight.

"Please write or email me," Cathy said.

Back at his house, Howard tip toed up the stairs and tapped on Clara's bedroom door.

She was awake and had been waiting for him to say goodbye.

"I'm leaving early in the morning, Mom."

Clara's eyes filled with tears. She was sending her oldest son off to the army, perhaps to fight and die.

"Take care of yourself, Howard. Continue to be the kind of good man that you are. Write," she said. "I'll miss you."

Howard bent and kissed her.

In their bedroom, Frank was still awake.

"I'll drive you to the recruiting station tomorrow morning," he said. "Sleep well." Frank had recently got his drivers license.

In the morning, before getting into the car, the brothers embraced.

At the recruiting station, Frank said," Good luck, Bro, " before he left.

The recruits were already boarding a small bus that would take them the short distance to the airport. Howard boarded the bus and found a seat next to Ramirez. He saw Lynch several seats away on the other side.

"How you doing, man?" Ramirez said with a smile.

"I'm O.K.," Howard said with a grin.

At the airport a plane awaited them.

"Where are we going?" one of the recruits asked the soldier who accompanied them.

"You're going to Fort Sill, Oklahoma," the soldier said. "That will be your new home for the next 10 weeks."

The flight lasted three hours with a stop over in Dallas, Texas. Flight attendants offered coffee and small pastries. Howard dozed, wondering what lay ahead for him. The plane landed in Lawson, Oklahoma where the recruits got on a bus that would take them to the base. Eventually the bus entered the front gate of Fort Sill.

6

Howard, along with the other recruits, was sent into a large hall and instructed to wait. There were no chairs or benches and after half an hour some of the men were sitting on the floor. A soldier entered the hall and in a loud voice, commanded, "On your feet!" The recruits stood.

"I'm Sergeant Chavez. For the next ten weeks I will be your platoon sergeant. You men are now recruits, but during the next ten weeks you will be turned into soldiers. Now I want you to form four ranks of twelve each."

After some confused shuffling around, the men stood in four ranks.

"As of this moment, you are now the Second Platoon of Charlie Company. Are there any questions?"

One of the men asked, "Sir, are we supposed to be at attention or at ease?"

"First of all, you don't address non-commissioned officers as 'Sir'. You say 'Sergeant'. And as far as your question, I will tell you when to be at attention. As a matter of fact, for the next ten weeks I will tell you what to do for most of your waking hours. Now, follow me. First rank, then second, and so on."

The sergeant led the platoon into another building resembling a huge barbershop and indeed six chairs waited for them each manned by a barber. In short order each recruit got a close military haircut. Using machine clippers, the process only took a few minutes.

When the entire platoon had been shorn, they were led by the sergeant into an adjoining building and ordered to take off all their clothes. The platoon then entered showers where hot water, soap, and towels were provided. The naked recruits were led through the brisk air to another building where they were issued underwear, socks, uniforms, and shoes. This process occupied most of an hour.

Sergeant Chavez ordered them outside and commanded them to "Fall in!" The recruits formed four ranks again. It was now midday, and the sergeant commanded, "Atten-shun! Right face! Forward march!" Chavez marched the platoon to the mess hall.

"O.K.," he said. "You have 30 minutes to get lunch, and then I want you to fall in again, right here. Dismissed!"

The mess hall resembled a cafeteria. Behind the counters, cooks stood with large portions of different types of food. Each recruit picked up a metal tray divided into compartments, and handed the tray to one of the cooks.

"What do you want?" the cooks asked, identifying the various foods. The filled tray was then handed back to the recruit who found a place at one of the tables. Howard found the food to be tasty, well cooked, and plentiful. Lemonade, ice tea, and coffee were available.

As he finished his lunch, Howard heard Sergeant Chavez call his name. "Private Frazer. Outside, now." Howard wondered what he had done wrong to be selected for a reprimand. He met the Sergeant in front of the mess hall.

"I heard there was a ruckus at the induction center between you and Private Lynch. What happened?" Chavez asked.

"Lynch started to hassle Ramirez, so I stopped him."

"You like Latinos?"

"I like most people except trouble makers," Howard said.

"Don't be one of those goody-goods. Just keep your nose clean and mind your own business." Chavez looked Howard over and felt his biceps. "You do sports, press iron, or something?"

Howard laughed. "No, when I was in high school, I worked part time in a hardware store jackassing heavy propane cylinders—carrying them out to customers' vehicles."

"Ever do any boxing?" Chavez asked.

Howard shook his head.

"I did some boxing before I entered the army," Chavez told him. "You know, Golden Gloves, stuff like that. I could give you a few pointers if you'd like."

"I'd like that, Sergeant," Howard said.

"O.K., I'll let you know. Now, fall in with the platoon."

Howard joined the rest of his platoon outside the mess hall where they gathered until Sergeant Chavez called out, "Second Platoon, fall in!"

The Sergeant marched the platoon to a medical building.

"Single file," Chavez commanded.

Nurses stood ready with syringes to administer injections.

"These shots are immunizations against a variety of infectious diseases," one of the nurses announced.

Someone called out, "Watch out for the square needle in your left nut!" which provoked a mixture of laughter and apprehension. Each recruit received four injections, two in each arm.

Afterward, Sergeant Chavez reformed the platoon and marched them to a barracks.

"Pick out a sack for yourselves," Chavez ordered. "You will be shown how to make up the bed. You are free for the rest of the day, but you must remain inside the barracks. Dismissed!"

Inside, Howard saw a large room filled with cots. At the foot of each cot was a small footlocker. A few soldiers circulated demonstrating how the cots were to be made up. Uniforms were to be stowed in the foot lookers.

Howard picked out a cot. He noticed some of the African Americans took cots near each other. Howard stretched out on his cot and wondered what the next day would bring.

In the late afternoon, Sergeant Chavez came in and announced, "You men are free to go to the mess hall for dinner after 1800."

Howard struck up a conversation with a recruit who occupied a cot near his.

"I'm Fred," he said, and they shook hands. Fred was from Alabama and spoke with a thick southern accent. At first Howard had trouble understanding him. They spent a long time talking with each other until Fred said, "I don't know about you, but I'm hungry. Let's go over to the mess hall and grab some chow."

Howard and Fred took trays and waited to select their food. As at lunch, the food tasted good to Howard.

"This is the best food I've had in a long time," Fred said, splashing ketchup on everything. Afterward, they strolled back to the barracks and talked until Taps sounded, and the lights were turned off. Howard lay on his cot thinking of his mother, Frank, and Cathy before he fell asleep.

7

Fort Sill, Oklahoma, January 2007

Howard was awakened at 0500 by a bugle call sounding Reveille, followed by a loud cannon shot, and the National Anthem played over loud speakers.

Sergeant Chavez entered the barracks to announce, "The Second Platoon will fall-in in 15 minutes."

Howard dressed hurriedly in the unfamiliar camos, rushed to the bathroom to brush his teeth and shave. He raced outside in time to fall in with the rest of the platoon. There were similar formations nearby. Sergeant Chavez called the platoon to attention.

"Listen up now. Those guys on our right are the First Platoon of Charlie Company. They're going to start morning exercises, and I want you all to do the same."

In short order the First Platoon started a series of vigorous exercises culminating in push-ups. Howard and the rest of his platoon struggled after five or six.

"Keep going," Sergeant Chavez said. "You'll be able to do a couple of hundred before we're through here."

When the exercises were completed, the platoon was dismissed to go back into their barracks and finish getting dressed. They were given a half hour for breakfast and then formed up again outside of their barracks. The rest of the day was occupied with classes on subjects including personal hygiene, avoiding sexually transmitted diseases, government insurance, the Uniform Code of Military Justice, Military Customs and Courtesy, sexual harassment, and equal opportunity.

During the afternoon, Sergeant Chavez took the platoon for a five mile run which left them gasping and dragging at the end.

Each day started with a morning routine that included warm-up, cardio, muscle, strength, and endurance exercises. In the afternoon, Chavez instructed them in Drill and Ceremony.

One evening, Sergeant Chavez told Howard, "Meet me at the gym near the NCO Club."

At the gym Chavez had two pairs of boxing gloves, one of which he laced on Howard's hands. They found an unoccupied ring and both climbed into it. Howard was somewhat nervous and didn't know what to expect.

Chavez showed Howard how to move his feet and how to use his arms to protect himself from opponents' blows.

"Most amateurs back away," Chavez told him. "What you need to do is get in close. Whenever you can, follow a left with a right."

Howard and Chavez spent several sessions together and after a few weeks, he told Howard, "You could be a fairly good boxer."

"Thanks, Sergeant. I appreciate the time you spent teaching me. I don't know when I'll ever get to use it, but . . ." he shrugged.

Not long after the boxing lessons, Howard strolled around the back of the mess hall waiting for dinner to begin. He sensed another soldier was following him. It was Private Lynch.

"I've been waiting for a chance to get you alone, Frazer," Lynch said, swinging a vicious punch at Howard's head. Howard's anger flared. As he learned from Sergeant Chavez, Howard blocked the blow, stepped in close, giving Lynch a hard left jab to his midsection. Lynch doubled-up, and Howard delivered a hard right punch to Lynch's head. Lynch fell.

"C'mon," Howard yelled, dancing around. "Get up unless you've had enough. I'm just getting warmed up."

Lynch was unable to stand, and Howard had to help him. "I guess I've had enough," he groaned. Howard's anger faded.

"You're lucky you didn't tangle with Ramirez," Howard told him. "He carries a switchblade sharp as a razor. He could open you up like a can of sardines. Better leave him alone."

"Yeah, I guess you're right," Lynch said. He looked around to see if anyone had observed their altercation, but they were alone.

"Where did you learn to fight?" Lynch asked, brushing some dirt from his camos.

"I got some pointers from Sergeant Chavez. He had you figured for a troublemaker. Let's get some chow," Howard said. Lynch grinned at Howard, and they entered the mess hall.

By the fifth week, weapons instruction started. The men were introduced to the M-16 rifle, learning to field strip, clean, and reassemble the weapon. This was followed by instruction in marksmanship. After several weeks the platoon was taken to the range where they fired at targets for qualification. Howard failed to achieve Expert Marksman, but qualified as a Sharp Shooter.

The men learned to use other weapons. They threw hand grenades, fired rifle grenades, sub-machine guns, and anti-tank weapons.

Howard's platoon took numerous long road and rough marches culminating in a 12- miler that lasted two nights and three days.

Howard received a letter from Frank with some bad news.

Dear Howard,

Mom hasn't been feeling well. She's had pain in her lower abdomen and has been bleeding. She went to the ER at UCONN. The doctor ordered a whole flock of tests including something called an endometrial biopsy. She'll return there next week. I'll keep you posted.

Frank

The letter worried Howard. *It sounds serious. Could be cancer.*

Howard also received a letter from Cathy. She asked about his progress and when he would be coming home.

Toward the end of the ten weeks, the recruits took a number of written tests to determine their eligibility for one of the military occupations or specialties. Howard scored high and chose 68W, a Healthcare Specialist. He wanted to be a combat medic.

Before graduation, Howard learned his choice had been approved, and he would go to Fort Sam Houston, Texas for 16 weeks of advanced training.

He called home and spoke to Frank. "How's Mom?"

"It doesn't look good," Frank told him. "Mom has stage three uterine cancer. She will start treatment next week with chemo and maybe radiation."

Howard was depressed by the news.

"How is she taking it?" he asked.

"You know Mom. She's holding up pretty well. She says she's going to fight it. How are you doing?" Frank asked.

"I'm doing O.K. I will finish basic training soon and be transferring to Fort Sam Houston, Texas. What are you up to?" Howard asked.

"I'm fine. My grades are good, and I'm making applications to some community colleges. I hope to get a scholarship, but I'm also checking out student loans."

"That's great, Frank. Keep up the good work. Keep me posted. Can I talk to Mom?"

Clara got on the phone.

"How are you, Howard? Is the army treating you well? Do they give you enough to eat?"

"I'm just fine, Mom, but I'm concerned about you. How are you feeling?"

"The pain is not too bad. I'm going to take the chemo and radiation treatment. Don't you worry about me. Take care of yourself," she said.

"I love you, Mom," Howard said before hanging up.

After she hung up, Clara thought about what she told Howard. *I know it's a bad disease, but I'll fight it as long as I can.*

During the graduation ceremony, Howard and his platoon stood at attention, watching the band march back and forth in front of the assembled troops. He reflected on how the past 10 weeks had turned them all into soldiers. *I learned how to march, to shoot, how to take care of myself and I am in good physical condition. I know about military courtesy and the Uniform Code of Military Justice. I am now a soldier, untested in battle, but trained and ready. Now, what I want is to become a medic.*

8

Fort Sam Houston, Texas, March 2007

Howard started his 16-week training as a Healthcare Specialist. He learned the duties of the 68W Specialty were not limited to treating battlefield casualties. His other duties included inpatient and outpatient care, preparing blood samples for the laboratory, and getting patients, operating rooms, equipment, and supplies ready for surgery.

There was a brief discussion of contagious diseases and the possible role of the military in helping to control epidemics. Howard learned of the world-wide flu pandemic in1923 and outbreaks of diseases such as Yellow Fever, Lassa Fever, Marburg Fever, and others including the 2001 outbreak of Ebola hemorrhagic fever in Uganda where 425 people were stricken resulting in 224 deaths.

He studied emergency patient care, how to sterilize surgical equipment, and techniques for applying plaster casts. Howard proved to be an apt student. He was surprised to find that his fingers, which he always thought of as clumsy, could learn to perform delicate tasks such as suturing wounds quickly and well. He looked forward to the opportunity to use his acquired skills.

Howard phoned home often to follow his mother's progress.

"Mom has started chemotherapy. It's making her sick," Frank said.

"It's the only way they can try to stop the cancer. Have her ask the doctors for medicine to help with the nausea," Howard said.

Howard's sixteen weeks at Fort Sam Houston seemed to race past. At graduation, he was promoted to Private First Class E3 and ordered to report to Walter Reed Army Hospital in Washington, D.C.

He took the next commercial flight to Washington. He had a window seat and was surprised when a young army nurse took the aisle seat alongside him. She was a second lieutenant.

After take off, a flight attendant asked the nurse for her drink order.

"Scotch on the rocks, please," she said.

"And you Sir?" the flight attendant asked Howard. He planned to order a beer but changed his mind. *If officers can drink scotch, why can't I?*

"The same for me," he said.

"Where are you heading?" the nurse asked.

"I'm going to D.C., where are you going, Ma'am?"

The nurse regarded Howard more closely. *He's no movie star, but looks like an okay guy.*

"I've been ordered to report to Walter Reed Army Hospital," she said.

"Same here, Lieutenant."

"Look, until we get there, let's forget the 'Ma'am' and 'Lieutenant' stuff. O.K.?"

Howard grinned at her. "Sure." He knew fraternization between officers and enlisted personnel was forbidden. This was the first time he had an unofficial conversation with an officer, in this case an attractive redhead, and he enjoyed it.

"What's your name?" she asked, smiling.

"Frazer, Howard Frazer."

"I'm Janet Jones. My friends call me 'J.J.' Where are you from?"

"Connecticut. Hartford, Connecticut," Howard said. "And you?"

"I grew up in Miami, Florida. My father is a psychiatrist there. Civilian," she added with a laugh.

Their drinks arrived. Howard lifted his drink and touched it to hers. *No clink with plastic,* he thought. *Maybe that's because she's an officer, and I'm enlisted.*

"Nice to meet you, J.J. Tell me about yourself."

"Sure. I went to the University of Florida in Gainesville and studied nursing. Then I joined the army, was commissioned, and here I am . . ."

"At 30,000 feet, talking to a PFC you just met," Howard continued. They both laughed. The flight attendant returned, and they ordered refills.

Howard liked J.J. and enjoyed talking with her.

"Is there a man in your life? Besides your father?" The second scotch somewhat loosened Howard's inhibition.

"Not one, but any number," she chuckled. "I'm free, and I want to stay that way for a while."

They continued the conversation throughout the flight. After landing and departing the plane, Howard said, "I think we can take the Metro to a station close to the hospital."

"Not me. I'm catching a cab. We can share it," J.J. said. Howard was about to demur, but she said, "No one will see us."

At the hospital, Howard tried to pay the taxi driver, but J.J. protested, and they split the fare. Before she got out, J.J. turned and kissed him on the lips.

"So long, Frazer. Maybe we'll see each other around."

"I'd like to see you again," Howard started to say, but she was already gone. *I've got to be quicker on the draw with this red head.*

9

Walter Reed Army Hospital, Washington, D.C., July 2007

Howard's first duties at Walter Reed Army Hospital were those of an orderly. He supplied bedpans and urinals to patients and helped prepare them for surgery. Later, he got operating rooms ready for surgery by sterilizing instruments in high-pressure steam autoclaves. Occasionally he caught a glimpse of J.J. When she saw him, she smiled and sometimes winked.

On a Friday afternoon, he got off duty at 4pm and took the Metro to Union Station. It was a warm day, and he decided to take a tour of the city. One of the companies offered double-decker open-air buses, and he bought a ticket with them. The tour would include all of the major tourist spots in Washington.

Howard found a seat on the upper deck of one of the buses. He enjoyed the sites when a familiar voice said, "Move your ass over, Frazer, and let me sit down."

Howard turned to see J.J. standing there. He smiled at her, "Have a seat, Lieutenant." Gesturing to the seat next to him. J.J. sat.

"We can't sit together, Howard," she said. "Somebody might report us. I'll sit on the other side, and when you decide to get off, I'll get off too, or you can get off when I do. Then we can decide about dinner."

Howard's mind reeled. *Decide about dinner? This woman moves fast.* He stayed on the bus for over two hours. When he got off at one of the tourist attractions, J.J. accompanied him. After viewing the Lincoln Memorial, Vietnam Memorial, the Air and Space Museum and a few others, they found themselves walking in the National Art Gallery.

"Where can we have dinner?" Howard asked her.

"We can't sit together in a restaurant," J.J. said.

"Then how . . . ?"

"I have an idea. I'm sharing a room with two nurses in a small hotel. They are both away on leave. We can go there and order room service. What about it?"

Howard did not hesitate. *Spending an intimate evening with this redhead sounds exciting.*

"Sure, let's go."

They took a taxi to Georgetown where J.J.'s hotel was located.

"My room number is 247. Don't be too long."

Howard waited in front of the hotel for fifteen minutes. *This looks like it will be fun.* He entered the hotel, walked to the second floor, found her room and knocked. J.J. opened the door, pretending to be surprised.

"Oh, Private Frazer. How nice to see you." She had already changed into jeans and a t-shirt revealing her shapely form. "Please come in."

She poured scotch into a glass with ice for him and one for herself.

"This time these will clink, " she said with a grin. "Get comfortable, Howard. Let's look at the menu."

They both decided on a steak dinner with a salad, potatoes, and a bottle of Bordeaux. J.J. called room service and placed the order.

"This beats what we usually get in the mess hall," Howard said, enjoying the steak and pouring more wine.

"And you don't have a gorgeous red head sitting next to you there either," J.J. quipped.

The wine bottle was soon empty. *Now what?* Howard thought.

"That was good," he said. "What's for dessert?"

J.J. smiled. "I'll show you." She took his hand and led him to the bedroom.

Howard picked her up, carried her to the bed, and started to kiss her.

"Get naked, Frazer," she whispered. "That's an order."

Howard had never gotten out of his uniform so fast. He lay naked on the bed and watched her remove her clothes, bra, and panties. He was ready for her when she slid into bed. She handed him a condom. He took her in his arms, but she rolled over and enveloped him. J.J. moaned and cried out as she climaxed, accompanied by Howard's loud "Ahhhh."

She rolled over and laid back, her head resting on his outstretched arm. Howard caressed her, kissing and gazing at her breasts and lower parts.

"Haven't you ever seen a naked woman?" she asked. In point of fact, Howard had not. His sexual adventures with Cathy had been managed in the dark rear seat of the family Toyota with both essentially completely clothed.

"Well, sure," Howard murmured.

"I'm getting hot again," J.J. moaned. Howard smiled at her. They continued making love until they both fell asleep.

In the morning J.J. asked, "When do you have to get back?"

"Monday morning," Howard told her.

"Great! We have the whole day. It's Saturday. Actually, we have two days." They made love again before J.J. called for breakfast. "We can't go out anywhere together," she said. "Someone could report us, and we'd both be in trouble. Of course, we could take another damn tour, but I'd rather stay here and fuck."

"Sounds good to me, J.J."

The next two days were an *mélange* of eating, drinking, and sex. J.J. showed Howard every position and technique she knew.

Howard couldn't believe it. *This woman is a three-ring circus. Are all women like this?*

During one joint shower, Howard made an effort at conversation. "Do you have any sibs?"

J.J. looked at him and laughed.

"No, I'm all that my father could handle. My mother divorced him when I was three. Let's get out now."

They toweled each other dry. *She dries me like someone would wipe down a horse.*

Their conversation was limited. Howard told her about his experience in basic training.

"We had this guy in our platoon who was a real trouble maker. For some reason, he had his eye on me. The sergeant gave me some boxing pointers. Then, sure enough, that guy jumped me, and I really decked him," Howard said with a laugh. "He didn't cause any trouble after that."

J.J. did not appear interested, but she felt his biceps.

"Wow," she said. She spoke about her amorous experiences in college with several fraternity members.

"Is there a special girl in your life?" J.J. asked.

"No, no one special."

"Want to watch TV?" J.J. asked.

"Why not?" Howard began to get bored.

Sunday evening, Howard climbed out of bed after their last encounter.

"I hate to end this, but I've got to get back," he said.

"Yeah, I know. Too bad." She watched him get dressed, pulled on a robe, and then walked him to the door.

"Will I see you again?" she asked.

"Not right away. I've put in for 5 days leave. My mother is sick. Uterine cancer."

"I'm sorry. That's a bad one."

"Yeah, I know. Well, anyway, I had a good time," he paused, somewhat embarrassed. "Look, I would like to pay for the meals." He reached for his wallet.

"Don't! I wouldn't feel right about it." J.J. smiled and kissed him. "You're a nice guy, Frazer. This was fun. Now get lost."

He smiled, saluted her, and left.

On the way back to his quarters, Howard thought about the weekend with J.J. *Having sex with a nurse - an officer—was a novelty. I think she just used me to satisfy her urges. Maybe our meeting on the bus was a coincidence, but after that, I think she had the whole thing planned. She has no feelings for me, not even friendly. She just used me like someone would rent a car—pick one out, use it, then return it. I wonder if she has done the same thing with other enlisted personnel? I feel sorry for her.* Howard was tired and by the time he fell into bed, he had stopped thinking about her.

10

Hartford, Connecticut, August 2007

Howard was granted 5 days leave and wasted no time in returning home. His mother was overjoyed to see him.

"You're looking good. The army must be treating you well," Clara said.

Howard was shocked to see how his mother had changed. *She looks so frail and weak. I think she's still in pain.*

Frank commented on the single chevron on Howard's sleeve.

"Looks like you've been promoted," he said, slapping Howard on the back.

"Yeah, I'm a PFC now. How are you doing?"

"I'm getting good grades," Frank told him. "I want to major in computer science. I hope to get a scholarship which will help pay my tuition."

"That's great," Howard said. *Frank is all wrapped up in himself. I'm disappointed that he didn't ask more about my life in the army. Oh well, he's just a kid.*

Later, Cathy came over to visit. She ran to Howard and hugged him.

"You look so handsome in your uniform," she gushed.

She has changed. Slightly taller and slimmer. More mature.

"How are things going, Cathy?" he asked.

"Oh, I'm still working in that fancy restaurant. It's just as a waitress for now, but I could move up to hostess. I'm taking courses at a community college. Learning to be a paralegal," she said. "How has the army been treating you?"

"Fairly well, I think. I'm learning a lot of new skills." *At least someone is interested in my life.*

"Are you free this evening? Maybe we could have dinner?"

"Sure, that would be fine."

Later when Howard picked her up he recognized things were different between them. His efforts to demonstrate affection somehow seemed awkward. *Things are different now. While we've been away from each other, we have changed. We're no longer adolescents. We've grown up.*

Over dinner, Cathy asked him about his plans for the future. "Are you going to make the army your career?"

"I might," he said. "It's not a bad life. Right now, I'm worried about my mother. Frank is so busy with his studies that he doesn't have time to keep me posted on her health."

"She doesn't look well," Cathy said. "I'll drop in to see her when I can and let you know how she's doing. She was there for me when I needed some advice that I couldn't get at home."

"Thanks, Cathy. I appreciate that."

"Howard, I need to tell you something. I'm seeing a couple of other guys. You know, socially. I wanted you to know."

"I figured you would," he said. "It's O.K., we're both free, but let's stay friends. I care about you." He thought of J.J. and how different these two women were.

"I'll always be your friend, Howard," she said.

Howard spent his time catching up on chores he used to do. He did some shopping for basics, mowed the lawn, got the screen door fixed, and had the car serviced. When his leave was over, Howard said goodbye to his mother. She looked at him like a drowning person might look at a possible savior.

"Take care of yourself, Howard," she said. "How will you get to the airport?"

"I'll take a cab. No problem." He hugged her. "I'll keep in touch."

In the taxi Howard wondered if he would ever see his mother again.

Back at Walter Reed, Howard resumed his duties. Occasionally he saw J.J. in a corridor. She smiled hurrying past him. *I'm not anxious to get involved with her.*

The assignment to Walter Reed was Howard's initial opportunity to practice the skills he learned at Fort Sam Houston. Furthermore, he definitely liked what he was doing, and for the first time he felt his work had a purpose other than financial. Howard always made an effort to do a good job and continued to do that in the army hospital. He was compassionate with his patients and performed his assigned tasks with alacrity and precision, receiving compliments on his performance from nurses, physicians, and patients.

Cathy sent letters reporting that Clara was responding well to the radiation and chemo. *I know it may only be temporary, but I'm happy for every day that she's alive and free of pain*, he thought.

Howard was selected to participate in a joint operation of the Department of Defense and the Federal Emergency Management Agency. In this program military and civilian hospitals were designated to receive both civilian and military patients in the event of a disastrous incident, natural or military, resulting in mass casualties.

Consideration was given to the possible victims of nuclear, chemical, or biological weapons. Volunteer civilian crews of surgeons, nurses, and technicians called Disaster Medical Assistance Teams would be organized, trained, and when deployed would rapidly travel to the disaster location. These DMATs would receive casualties, perform triage, stabilize them, and arrange for their transport to designated hospitals. At Walter Reed, Howard, with other Healthcare Specialists, was responsible for the reception of these casualties. The patients would be re-triaged and delivered to the appropriate section in the hospital depending on the nature of their wound or disease. The organization, actual operation, and the "after–ops" analysis of this program took six months.

March 2008

Howard returned to his regular assigned duties at Walter Reed.

In his free time, he continued to explore Washington. The weather was mild, and sometimes he rode in a bus, hoping he would not encounter J.J. On one Saturday afternoon, he decided to visit the National Gallery of Art located on the Mall. Once there, he strolled through the Sculpture Garden pausing to admire the statues and other artistic structures of glass and metal. Afterwards, he walked to the terrace where he saw a number of artists sketching or painting. A young woman attracted his attention. She was seated before an easel and used a palette of paints. She wore a light colored hat with a wide floppy brim. He stood a few paces behind her and watched as she painted her version of the scene. After observing her for some time, he ventured to say, "It's wonderful how you can do that. Do you come here often?"

She turned to look at him. He saw that she was Asian. Her face was pale with wide set brown eyes and long eyelashes. Her black hair was tied in a ponytail. She was beautiful. She regarded Howard for a moment or two.

"Yes, quite often," she said before returning to her painting. Her voice was low and sweet. *She looks like a painting herself.*

Howard swallowed. He did not know what to say. He continued to watch her for fifteen minutes and said, "Have a nice day," before strolling away.

That night, lying in bed, Howard thought about the young artist before sleep claimed him.

11

The following day Howard wanted to return to the National Gallery of Art. *I wonder if that Oriental girl will be there?*

Arriving at the Gallery, he walked to the terrace, searching for her among the other artists. He found her not far from where she had been yesterday still painting the same scene.

Howard continued to watch in silence. He was impressed with how she moved her brush over the palette picking up several colors to blend them as she transferred them to her canvas.

When she noticed him, he smiled at her and said, "Hi. I hope I'm not getting too personal, but where did you learn to paint so beautifully?"

The young woman put her brush down and turned to face him, and said, "I started to paint in China, but I was fortunate enough to obtain a scholarship here at the American University College for the Arts.

"How long have you been here?" Howard asked.

"Just over a year," she said.

"Can I introduce myself?" he asked.

She smiled and nodded.

"I'm Howard Frazer. I work here at Walter Reed Army Hospital. Can I ask your name?"

"My name is Mei Li Chen. You are a soldier?"

"Yes. I trained to help sick and wounded soldiers."

Her face brightened. "That's good. My father hates soldiers. He remembers the revolt when soldiers killed hundreds of civilians in Tiananmen Square in Beijing."

Mei Li wore a smock with occasional paint smears over a light cotton dress. The day was warm.

"I'm going inside the gallery to look around for a while," he said. "Maybe when I'm finished, you would join me for a cool drink?" he asked.

"Thank you. That might be pleasant."

Howard walked into the gallery and spent an hour or so admiring paintings. Around noon he returned to the terrace to find her. He hoped she would still be there. *Maybe I came on too strong, and she left.* Then he saw where she was and hurried over to her.

"Shall we go?" he asked.

Mei Li rose. She was half a head shorter than he was. She gathered her things together. Howard carried the folded stool and easel. They walked to an outdoor café near the gallery. Howard asked for iced tea.

"If you don't mind," she said, "I'd prefer hot tea."

"I'll have that, too," he told the waiter. "Would you like something to eat?" the waiter asked.

"I have a sandwich," she said. Howard ordered a sandwich for himself.

"How long will you remain in the U.S.?" he asked. Mei Li's face clouded.

"I don't know. My father keeps writing to me. He wants me to return to China."

"Why?"

"Because there is a man there whom my father wants me to marry."

"Do you know this man?" Howard asked.

"Yes, I met him a few times."

Howard was not sure how to ask . . ."Did he . . . I mean did you agree to marry him?"

"No, but he comes from a good family, he has money, and my father is anxious for me to marry him.

I don't want to. At this point of my life, I'm only interested in painting." She changed the subject. "Do you like art, Howard?" she asked.

"Yes, but I don't know anything about it."

"Tell me about yourself," she said.

Howard told her about growing up in Connecticut with his mother and brother. After half an hour, Mei Li stood. "Thank you for the tea, Howard. I have to go now."

"Can I walk with you to where you live?" Howard asked. "I can help carry your stuff."

"Yes, if you wish. I live nearby, but I can manage quite well."

Crossing the Mall, they reached a small rooming house.

"This is where I live. I share a room here with two other girls."

"I'd like to see you again, Mei Li." Howard said.

"I paint at the gallery almost every day. It was nice meeting you, Howard." She turned and entered her house.

I like her. She is the first woman who showed any interest in me. She's talented, but sad. I don't think she is anxious to go back to China and marry that man.

The following Saturday Howard spotted Mei Li on the terrace and walked over to her.

"Hi. How are you today?" he asked.

"I'm fine, thank you," she said with a smile. "I found what you told me yesterday very interesting. I'd like to learn more about you. Tell me about your childhood. I can listen while I paint."

He told her about working part time during high school, about Frank, and the difficulty of finding a job. He did not mention Cathy.

"I even tried to become a plumber," he laughed.

"Why did you become a soldier?"

"I couldn't find a decent job. The army offered a career, and I took it. I like working with doctors and nurses helping sick or wounded soldiers."

"What will you do if they send you to fight in the Middle East?"

"I will have to go. I'm a soldier, and I must follow orders, but I hope I won't have to go and fight."

It started to rain. Mei Li hurriedly gathered up her things, and they rushed to go inside the Gallery. Once inside and out of breath, they laughed, as the rain became a downpour. Mei Li checked her painting supplies.

"Let's walk. What would you like to see?" she asked.

"I don't know, but I want to learn. Show me the things you like."

Mei Li smiled, and took his hand. For the rest of the day, she introduced him to the Dutch Masters, French Impressionists, and the Modernists. They stopped only to have a snack at the Gallery's Café. *This is interesting. She knows so much about painting. It's fun to be with her.*

12

Howard spent most of his free time with Mei Li. Every Saturday morning he hopped on a tour bus that would take him to the National Gallery of Art. On one such morning, he was on the upper level of the tour bus watching the sights go by when he heard a familiar voice.

"Hi Howard. I see you're still touring the city." He turned to see J.J. sitting on the opposite side.

"Nice to see you again, Lieutenant," he said.

"I haven't seen you in a long time. Where have you been hiding?" she asked.

"I was involved with that D.O.D.–F.E.M.A. program", he said.

"I happen to be free today," she said. "Would you like to join me for lunch? You know like we did the other time?"

That is the last thing I want to do. "I'd really like to, Lieutenant, but I can't. I already have a date. With a civilian," he added.

J.J. looked as if she had been struck on the head. She managed a weak smile.

"O.K.," she said. "It's your loss." The next time the bus stopped, she got up, gave him a wave, and left the bus.

That evening J.J. sat morosely at a table in the O Club when Carol, one of her nurse roommates, came over and joined her.

"What's wrong, J.J.? You look like you just missed your flight."

"It's that new guy, PFC Frazer, the one I've been seeing on the QT. I asked him for a date, and he turned me down. This is the first time a man has ever opted out for a date with me."

Carol laughed. "That's tough titty. Let me buy you a drink."

Howard could not help comparing Mei Li's quiet, shy personality with that of the aggressive army nurse. Seeing Mei Li pushed all thoughts of J.J. from his mind.

Mei Li introduced Howard to her friends, all of who were Chinese. They were polite, but continued to speak to Mei Li in Chinese. Howard was certain that they were talking about him. He was jealous of her friendly interaction with them and wanted to have her to himself. Mei Li sensed his discomfort and said, "Let's get some lunch. I know a restaurant that serves great *dim sum."*

Howard did not know what *dim sum* was, but he was happy to go with her.

It was Sunday, and the restaurant was crowded. They found an empty table and soon a Chinese waitress wheeled a cart bearing multiple small dishes of the Chinese treats up to them. Mei Li pointed to a number of these dishes, and the waitress placed them on their table before pushing her cart to other customers.

"This is the way they serve these snacks in China," Mei Li said.

"Some of them are filled with pork, some with shrimp, and others with vegetables." Bowls of dipping sauces sat on the table. "You just pick up a dumpling, dip it in the sauce and eat. Each sauce has a different flavor."

Howard tried one using the chopsticks. "Um, this is delicious," he said, reaching for another dish. They washed the *dim sum* down with hot tea. In a few minutes they had finished all the dishes. Mei Li signaled for the waitress to come by again with her cart so they could select more of the delicacies. When they had eaten enough, Mei Li asked a waiter for the check. He just counted the empty dishes on their table and handed the check to Howard.

"How did he know what we ate?" Howard asked her.

Mei Li laughed. "They all cost the same."

Walking from the restaurant she asked him, "What would you like to do now, Howard?"

"I'd like to go back to the gallery with you and learn more about art."

As they walked back, Howard said, "What is there about painting that pleases you?"

"I like creating, " she said. "When I see something beautiful, a landscape or a seascape, I try to capture it with my paintbrush and hope that others might find the painting pleasing. That is what gives me pleasure."

"Creating is a special talent. Not everyone has it," Howard said.

Mei Li said, "Some of those who have it are called artists."

On their way to Mei Li's apartment, Howard took her hand.

They continued hand in hand until they reached her front door.

"Would you like to see the cherry blossoms?" she asked. "They are out now."

"Yes, I would. That sounds great."

"I'll pick you up Saturday morning," he said. He still held her hand. "I'd like to kiss you," he said.

Mei Li smiled. "That's what I like about you, Howard. Most men just 'take', you ask." She put her arms around his neck and gave him a lingering kiss. Her lips were soft. "See you next Saturday," she said and entered her house.

The week seemed to drag for Howard. He thought of Mei Li as he performed his duties. At night he dreamed of her.

Saturday was bright and sunny. He and Mei Li took a cab to the Tidal Basin and strolled around admiring the blossoms. They passed a sign indicating that the trees were a gift from Japan in 1912 commemorating the friendship between the two countries.

"And then forty years later they bomb Pearl Harbor," Howard said. "But now we are friends again, after we nuked Hiroshima and Nagasaki. It's a crazy world."

"The Japanese invaded China in 1931 and stayed for ten years," Mei Li said. "We called the Japanese the 'ocean dwarves' and they refer to us as the 'garlic eaters'. We always hated each other."

They visited the Lincoln Memorial where Howard told her about slavery and the Civil War.

"I think Abraham Lincoln was a great president," Mei Li said.

"So do I. Slavery is a terrible thing. I believe all men should be free."

13

During the following months, Howard took Mei Li to movies, a concert, and to see the Washington Nationals play baseball.

On one occasion, Howard said, "I want to ask you about nudes. How is it that all the paintings of nudes I've seen were all female? Does anyone paint male nudes?"

"Until recent times, almost all artists were men. Men like to look at women so they painted the female body."

"So that means the men decided what art should be?"

Mei Li grinned at him.

"You are very perceptive, Howard. But now women are becoming artists, and there are some famous ones, like Grandma Moses and Georgia O'Keeffe."

She took Howard to Chinese restaurants, and he found the food to be delicious. She loved barbecue and baby back ribs.

Howard was in love. One evening he asked, "How do you say 'I love you' in Chinese?"

Mei Li blushed.

"You say 'Wau ai nee'," she said.

Howard turned her face to his and kissed her.

"Wau ai nee."

Mei Li laughed at his pronunciation. "I love you, too," she said.

"I wish there was someplace where we could be alone," he said.

"I have to tell you that I had a letter from my father urging me to come home. He wrote about honor and family." Tears came into her eyes. "It's very hard for me, Howard."

He took her into his arms and held her close.

"Please don't go, Mei Li. Stay here with me. I want to marry you. I'll make you happy."

"How can you marry me?" Mei Li sobbed. "You are in the army, and I don't want to be a soldier's wife. You could be sent to Iraq and be killed."

"I won't always be in the army," Howard said. "My enlistment has only three years left."

"I don't know," Mei Li said. She kissed him, and they parted.

The next day, Howard received orders transferring him to a combat unit at Fort Drum in New York State near the Canadian border.

He barely had time to take a taxi to the National Gallery of Art, find Mei Li on the terrace, and say a hurried goodbye.

"I'll write to you as soon as I get there," he said. He kissed her and rushed to the waiting taxi.

Fort Drum, New York, November 2008

Howard arrived at his new base. A sign at the gate read "The Home of the 10th Mountain Division." He reported to headquarters and found the duty sergeant.

"PFC Frazer, reporting for duty."

The sergeant consulted his computer. "You mean Corporal Frazer," he said.

"No," Howard said. "I'm a PFC."

"You've been promoted. You're a corporal now. Now you can use the Non-Commissioned Officer's Club."

Howard learned he was assigned as a combat medic to Bravo Company, 2nd Battalion, 1st Brigade Combat Team, 10th Mountain Division.

He found his quarters and settled in. The men in his company were glad to have him.

"We might be needing a medic before long," one of them said.

They knew sooner or later they would be deployed to Iraq.

Bravo Company honed their military skills during many combat exercises, but Howard had little opportunity to practice his medical talents. His mind was occupied with Mei Li.

A few days before they shipped out, Howard received a letter from Mei Li. It was postmarked Shanghai. He opened it with a sinking heart.

Dear Howard,

I had to return to China because my father was ill. I must tell you that I'm going to marry the man my father chose for me. I love you and will always remember you. As you said, at the Cherry Blossom Festival, it's a crazy world."

Mei Li Chen

Howard became despondent. He knew he would never see Mei Li again.

In January 2009, the 1st Brigade Combat Team, including Bravo Company, was deployed to Iraq.

14

Hartford, Connecticut, February 2010

Frank prepared to graduate from college. He now had a new group of friends, fellow students and often went out with them for a boisterous evening of drinking. One friend, Randy Babcock, invited him to a party.

"My parents have a big house in Avon. They will be away for the weekend. We can have a blast."

By the time Frank arrived the party was well underway. Inside Frank could smell marijuana mixed with tobacco smoke.

Randy saw him and greeted him.

"Hey, Frank! Glad you could come. The booze is in the kitchen. Help yourself."

It was obvious that Randy already had had a few drinks. Frank found a bottle of rum and used it to spike a coke. It tasted good to him, and he made another for himself before joining the others. He was surprised to see Cathy there.

"Hi Cathy, nice to see you again. I didn't know you knew Randy."

"I don't. One of my girlfriends knows him. How are you, Frank?"

"I'm good," he said. "What's new?" His words were already slurred.

"Nothing much. I'm still working as a waitress, but I'm taking some courses. You want to dance?"

Frank parked his drink and joined her in the dance. The music was loud rock and like the others, he started to twist and gyrate, taking her hand to draw her close. He could smell her perfume.

Eventually, Cathy said, "I'm starved. Let's get something to eat."

They retrieved cold slices of pizza and sat on the couch eating, watching the others.

One of Frank's friends smoked a cigarette, obviously not tobacco. He came over to Frank and Cathy.

"Want a toke?" he asked them.

Frank took a deep drag and offered the joint to Cathy. Taking care not to wet the joint, she took a deep drag, held it as long as she could, then handed it back to Frank. He took another drag before returning the joint to his friend.

The party went on for hours. Randy saw Frank and Cathy both asleep on the couch.

He woke them. "You're in no shape to drive," he told Frank. "You can crash here. There are plenty of beds upstairs."

Cathy learned that her friend had left the party without her.

Frank and Cathy went upstairs, found a room with twin beds and fell into them. Sometime during the night, Cathy woke to find Frank in her bed.

"This isn't your bed," she said.

"I know," Frank said. "But we're friends."

After brief consideration, Cathy agreed. "That's true, we are."

April 2010

Cathy often stopped over for a visit to see how Clara faired.

Clara was in remission and feeling better since completing her treatment.

On this day Cathy saw Frank and said, "I need to speak with you privately."

"I don't have any time now. I'm on my way to class."

"It's important," Cathy said. "We need to talk now."

"O.K., O.K., make it fast."

They walked to Frank's room. Cathy closed the door and said, "I'm pregnant."

"Who's the father?" Frank asked with a smirk.

Cathy was not amused. "That's not funny," she said. "You are."

Frank became defensive. "How do I know that?"

"Because you are the only man I had sex with since Howard left for the army."

"So you say. What do you want from me?"

"It would be nice if you showed some responsibility. What should I do?" Cathy became upset.

"You need to have an abortion."

"Abortions are expensive. I don't have that much money."

"How much do they cost?" he asked.

"The one I found out about costs $500. You've got to help me, Frank."

"What do you mean 'I've got to'?" he said.

"If you don't help me, I'm going to tell your mother."

This is the last thing I need. It could kill Mom.

"O.K., O.K.," Frank said. "I'll meet you tomorrow in the college library at three o'clock, and I'll give you the money. Now I've got to go." He opened the door, walked downstairs, and left the house leaving her standing in his room. Cathy began to cry. She wept silently for five minutes, not wanting Clara to hear her. She found a tissue, dried her eyes and, after changing her expression, went downstairs to say goodbye to Clara.

The following day Cathy went to the library. She got there thirty minutes early and waited for Frank, but he failed to appear. She spent a miserable day at work, hoping for a call from Frank. *What will I do if he doesn't give me the money?* Finally she reached Frank by phone.

"I went to the library, but I didn't see you," he lied. "I thought maybe you changed your mind," Frank said.

"I was there and waited two hours," she said. "But you never came. I'm coming over tonight to tell your mother."

"O.K., O.K.," Frank said. "Where can we meet?"

"You can bring the money to me at the restaurant tomorrow," she said.

Cathy watched for Frank all day while working. He appeared in the late afternoon and surreptitiously handed her an envelope. Frank started to leave, but she caught hold of his sleeve.

"Wait a minute," she said and tore open the envelope.

"There's only $300 here," she whispered. Diners at tables were beginning to stare at them.

"That's all I can get," Frank said and walked out of the restaurant.

Cathy became desperate. That night she confessed her condition to her parents. They were not sympathetic. Her mother screamed and cried. Her father ranted and raved, called her a slut, and ordered her out of the house.

Cathy spent the night with one of her girlfriends who cried and sympathized with her. In the morning Cathy was resolute. She returned to her parents' apartment and demanded $200 from her mother. Cathy had been contributing a major portion of her salary to her parents each week. She packed a small suitcase with her clothes, personal effects, and left the apartment. She did not plan to return.

May 2010

Frank graduated from the community college after two years studying computer technology. Clara was determined to give Frank a party and asked for a list of his friends. She also invited her friends, Cathy and some of the neighbors. Clara wished Howard could come. She sent these invitations by email. Everyone accepted except Cathy who sent her regrets. Clara ordered platters of food, wine, beer, and soft drinks and a graduation cake.

Clara watched Frank receive an Associate Degree in Computer Science.

"What now?" one of Frank's friends asked.

"I need to find a job," Frank said. "Something with computers. I've sent out resumes and I'm waiting to hear."

"Do you ever see Cathy? Did you know that she's living in West Hartford?"

"No, I never see her. I didn't know she moved."

15

June 2010

Frank got a phone call from a company asking him to come for an interview. The company, Spenser Corporation, was located in downtown Hartford. George Spenser, the president, met him.

After a lengthy interview, Spenser said, "We are a small company. Why do you want to work for us rather than with a large IT company?"

"I thought that in a smaller company, there would be more opportunity for me to learn and grow. Also, your company is close to where I live."

Spenser gave Frank a tour of the facility. Frank could see there were about twenty-five employees in individual cubicles. He noted that the equipment appeared to be up to date. The tour concluded in Spenser's office.

"Our company specializes in tech support for individuals and companies. We are relatively small, but concentrate on aiding those who can use our skills and experience. Our clients range from individuals with a one time glitch or technical problem to those who have contracted with us for ongoing support. Your specialty studies in computer technology should be a good fit here."

"I would be extremely interested in working for you, Mr. Spenser. I'm sure I have a lot to learn."

Spenser, a man in his sixties with graying hair, considered Frank for a minute or two. He smiled.

"Well, Frank, we will give you a try." Spenser told him what the starting salary would be and indicated a vacant cubicle. "This will be your space." He introduced Frank to a young man in the adjoining cubicle. "This is Robert O'Neal. Bob will help you get started. See you Monday morning."

Frank thanked him and couldn't wait to tell Clara that he had found a job. The salary was more than he expected.

December 12, 2010

Frank did exceptionally well at Spenser Corporation. His co-worker, Bob O'Neal, helped him get started. Frank was a quick learner, and after his first three months, George Spenser entered his cubicle to remark, "You are doing just fine. Several clients have called me to say how patient and efficient you were handling their problem. Some also mentioned they liked dealing with you. Keep up the good work." At his 6-month review, Frank was praised again for the quality of his work and received a raise.

Frank was elated. He decided to go out with three of his friends to celebrate. They met at a bar and sat in a booth ordering beer and bar snacks. A large TV showed a football game in progress. The game went into overtime, and by the time it ended, much beer had been consumed. It was time to leave.

"Hey Frank, are you O.K. to drive?" one of his friends asked.

"Yeah, I'm fine."

But Frank was not fine. He realized he was significantly drunk. *I have to get home. I promised Mom I would be home before midnight. I'll be careful.*

Frank drove the old Toyota. He drove fast, faster than usual. Without realizing it, he speed through the streets at sixty miles per hour. His driving became erratic.

Earlier that evening in a ground floor apartment a tragedy began to unwind when Emily Cordova and her mother sat down to have supper. Emily, five years old, cradled Raggedy Ann, her favorite doll, as her mother accidently knocked over an open bottle of hot pepper oil spilling some of the oil on the doll. Emily began to cry and reached for the doll to embrace it. In a movement as swift as a striking serpent, Mrs. Cordova snatched the doll from Emily interrupting the child's move to bring the doll to her face sparing her daughter a possible excruciating episode of the oil entering her eyes.

"I want my Raggedy Ann," the child wailed.

"Don't cry *Querida*," her mother said. "I'll buy you another doll tomorrow." But Emily sobbed as the doll went into the garbage.

When the meal was over, a sobbing Emily saw her mother tie up the plastic bag containing the day's garbage and the doll, preparing to dispose of it. She watched out the window as her mother took the bag outside to throw it into a garbage can inside a wooden bin. These bins had been placed there by the city to protect the garbage from the depredation of scavenging rodents and other vermin.

After Emily was put to bed, she wept into her pillow for a long time. She loved her Raggedy Ann doll with its wide-open eyes and painted smile and was determined to retrieve it. When she thought her mother had gone to sleep, Emily tiptoed out the door, shaking with cold as she crossed the street. She opened the bin and went inside to find her Raggedy Ann. At that moment, Frank swerved around a corner at high speed, striking and demolishing the wooden bin. Inside the bin, Emily was killed by the impact.

"Holy shit," he exclaimed. "What the hell have I done?"

Lights appeared in the windows of neighboring homes.

I'd better get out of here right away. He did not know he had just killed a child. He backed away from the wrecked bin and sped off with screeching tires. *I've got to hide this car somewhere before Mom sees this. Someplace I can get it fixed—a place where the cops won't see it.*

Frank drove for several miles past the city limits until he located a small auto repair shop. He parked in front, waiting for it to open. He sat in the car for many hours, dozing now and then, until the shop opened at eight o'clock.

"I've had a slight fender bender," Frank told the repairman. "I don't want my mother to see the damage. No one was hurt, but I'd like to keep it out of sight until you finish fixing it. I don't want to report it to the insurance or anything. How much is this going to cost me?"

The repairman smelled the beer on Frank's breath. He examined the damage.

"The repair, including repainting, will run you about $2,700. Keeping it out of sight will cost you an extra 300 bucks."

Frank agreed and started to walk the miles back home.

16

December 13, 2010, 5:30 a.m.

Mrs. Cordova went into the kitchen to prepare breakfast. An hour later, she called, "Emily. Breakfast." When the child did not appear, Mrs. Cordova went into Emily's room to wake her, but the child was gone. The bedclothes were cold. *Maybe she is hiding*. Mrs. Cordova searched the small apartment calling, "Come out Emily. Breakfast is getting cold." Mrs. Cordova became frightened. *She has been kidnapped!* She rushed to the phone and called 911.

"My child has been kidnapped," she told the dispatcher. "She's five years old. Please find her, hurry!" She gave her name and address.

Across the street a group of neighbors stood looking at the shattered bin. There was a strong stench of garbage.

"He must have been doing about seventy-five," one of the onlookers said. A police car pulled up in front of the apartment house. One of the officers got out and went in to talk to Mrs. Cordova. The other officer walked over to the bin to investigate. At that moment, a woman peered into the bin and saw the child's body. "It's little Emily!" she screamed. The officer went upstairs and whispered to his partner, talking to a distraught Mrs. Cordova. Now the officers asked Mrs. Cordova to accompany them across the street to the bin. "Is that your daughter?" one of the officers asked. Mrs. Cordova looked once, then shrieked, "*Dios mio*!" and fainted.

By eight o'clock more police had arrived together with an ambulance, and at least one of the TV stations was filming the scene. Mrs. Cordova, now revived, attempted to answer questions.

"I don't know how my baby got into that bin," she said between sobs. "Emily was a good girl."

None of the neighbors had seen Frank's car.

Frank saw the story about the accident on the morning news as he dressed. *Oh my God, what have I done? I killed a little girl*. The story related how incensed neighbors were collecting money as a reward for information leading to the arrest of the perpetrator.

Frank took a bus to work, arriving late. He was barely able to function. Several of his fellow workers noted his distressed demeanor and asked if he was all right.

"Nothing. No problem. I just had a bad night," Frank muttered.

The auto repairman also watched the morning news. The story showed the smashed shed. He became suspicious and notified the police. A policeman came to the repair shop and examined Frank's car. The registration was in the glove compartment.

"I don't want to get in trouble," the repairman told the officer.

"He offered me extra money to keep it quiet, and he smelled like a brewery."

"Thank you," the officer said. "We'll take it from here."

Frank returned home from work that day. He was eating dinner when there was a knock at the door. Clara was upstairs.

"I'll get it," Frank called and walked to the door to find a police officer.

"Are you the owner of a 2001 Toyota?" the officer asked.

Frank felt panic rising within him. "No, it's my mother's car."

"Are you aware the car was involved in an accident resulting in the death of a child?"

"No—well, yes, I saw it on TV."

"Who drives that vehicle?" the policeman asked.

"Well, actually my mother, me and my brother."

"Were you driving the car last night?"

"No. It must have been my brother, Howard," Frank said. *Howard is safe, away in the army so they can't touch him.*

"Where is your brother now?"

"He's away in the army."

"Away in the army where?" the officer asked. "If he's away in the army, how could he have driven the car?"

Frank did not reply.

"O.K.," the officer said, "we'll be back."

The next evening, the same police officer came to Frank's house. "I'm placing you under arrest for D.U.I., vehicular homicide, and leaving the scene of an accident."

"I told you I didn't do it, it was my brother," Frank protested.

"The repairman where you brought the vehicle contacted us. He is prepared to identify you and to testify in court." The policeman handcuffed Frank and read him his rights.

"Can I just tell my mother?" Frank asked. The policeman escorted him into the house and into the dining room.

"What's happening?" Clara asked. "Why have you handcuffed my son?"

"He is under arrest for vehicular homicide," the policeman said.

"I'm sorry, Mom. I was in an accident. A little girl was killed. I didn't know it at the time—I only found out about it the next day."

"Oh, my God!" Clara exclaimed.

"Can you get me a lawyer?" Frank asked as he was led away.

At the police station, Frank was booked and put into a cell where he spent the night. He didn't sleep. *What's going to happen to me?*

17

The following morning a man entered Frank's cell.

"I'm Martin Levine, your lawyer," he said handing Frank his card. "Your mother contacted me." The lawyer pulled up a chair, and Frank sat on his cot facing him.

"Tell me the whole story," Levine said.

Frank told him everything.

"The police report states that you tried to blame your brother Howard for the accident. Is that true?"

Frank nodded.

"Why did you do that?"

"I was scared. I was just playing for time. Howard's name came into my head."

"O.K.," Levine said, "I'll have you out of here in an hour or so, then come to my office, and we'll talk."

After Frank was released, he went home to tell his mother and explained, in detail, about the accident.

"I know I shouldn't have done it," he said. "I drank too much beer and—I got drunk."

Clara started to cry. "What will happen to you?"

"I don't know. I've got to see the lawyer now."

Following his visit to Mr. Levine, Frank went to see Mr. Spenser. In Spenser's office, Frank told him about the accident.

"I'm out on bail now, but I'm sure I will be convicted. I just wanted to tell you how sorry I am it happened. I really enjoyed working here."

Spenser was shocked by Frank's admission. "Young man," Mr. Spenser said, looking grim, "this is a terrible thing, the killing of a young child. However, I appreciate your honesty in telling me about it. When this is all settled, come back and see me. It's just possible there could still be a place here for you."

Spenser was a widower. His wife died early in their marriage leaving him to raise their daughter. He spent most of his waking hours developing the business. He valued honesty and sincerity as important qualities and tried to inculcate them in his employees.

January 3, 2011

Martin Levine was able to have the charge of vehicular homicide reduced to involuntary manslaughter. Frank pleaded guilty to all the charges and was sentenced to eighteen months in prison and a $5,000 fine. He was sent to a minimum-security facility in Connecticut used to house white-collar criminals.

On arrival the warden warned him, "Any misbehavior and you will be sent to the Northern Correctional Facility. That's where the bad guys are."

A guard issued ill-fitting prison garb to Frank, but he was not confined in a cell. The guards were unarmed. One of the guards took him aside and said, "I can arrange for you to have better fitting clothes and someone to make your bed every day. I can also arrange overnight conjugal visits at a motel."

"What do I have to do to enjoy those benefits?" Frank asked.

"Just arrange to have a $100 mailed to my wife every month," the guard said.

"Unfortunately, I can't afford those pleasures," Frank told him. "I'll have to do it the hard way."

But life was not hard for Frank. It never had been. He was able to jog and even found a tennis partner. Other inmates entertained themselves in different ways. One of them gave a course in arson. Another inmate described the technique of lock picking. Most of the men did not talk about their crimes, but those who did usually indicated they would not repeat them.

At night when Frank lay in his cot, he could not get over his feelings of guilt and remorse over little Emily and Clara. *My reckless behavior caused the death of an innocent little girl. This prison sentence and the fine do not make up for that. I can never forget what I did.* Frank often cried himself to sleep. He resolved that for the rest of his life he would be a more thoughtful and considerate person.

Clara's symptoms returned. The visiting nurse suggested that Clara go to the hospital where it was determined that further chemotherapy or radiation would not be helpful. Pain management was the only modality to be used, and the visiting nurse arranged for Clara to be transferred to a hospice managed by the Catholic Church. The visiting nurse was able to get a message to Frank that his mother was in hospice care.

Clara was worried about her sons. *Howard is in Iraq. How will he react if he finds out that Frank tried to blame him for the accident? I heard what Frank said to the police when they came to arrest him. And now poor Frank is in prison.* Clara sent word to Attorney Martin Levine that she wanted to make a will.

Cathy learned from neighbors that Clara was now in a hospice. She decided to visit Clara, who told her about her sons.

"Howard is fighting in Iraq, and Frank is in prison," Clara said.

"It must be hard for you being alone with neither of your sons able to visit," Cathy said. "I will write to them and let them know how you are doing."

Clara thanked her.

But the only letter Cathy wrote was to Howard. She told him that his mother was presently in a hospice being given enough medication to keep her free of pain. She also wrote that Frank had been convicted and was now in prison.

Frank was told that the warden wanted to see him.

"I'm afraid I have some bad news for you," the warden said.

"Your mother has been transferred to a hospice. They keep her as pain free as possible."

"Thank you," Frank said. "I know about that. The visiting nurse was able to get a message to me."

"I'm sorry," the warden said.

Frank returned to his room in dejection. At night, he wept quietly into his pillow, thinking of his dying mother and wishing he could be with her.

18

Iraq, January 2011

Howard had been in Iraq with Bravo Company for two years. Clara wrote to tell him about Frank's accident and arrest. She told him Frank had been arrested for drunk driving, leaving the scene of an accident, and vehicular homicide. He was presently out on bail. She did not tell Howard Frank had accused him of the crime when he was arrested.

Jesus Christ, how could my kid brother do such a stupid thing? I wish I could be there to help him, but there's nothing I can do about it.

Bravo Company was billeted near an Iraqi Army brigade. The mission of the 1st Combat Brigade, of which Bravo Company was a part, was to provide training and support to the Iraqi troops. For many months, Howard's unit tried to teach the Iraqis and encourage them in their effort to contain the rebels and Al Qaida. Howard found the Iraqi soldiers to be pleasant and anxious to learn but not enthusiastic about fighting.

Bravo Company was assigned to help drive the Al Qaida from a number of villages. During these brief combat episodes, Bravo Company pursued the Al Qaida, firing on them when feasible. Howard felt no animosity toward the enemy. *I am a professional soldier doing my job. I am sorry for these civilians, the men, women, and children who are often caught in an exchange of fire between the rebels and us.*

Missions took place over a period of months and thus far, Bravo Company had not experienced any casualties.

A week later their luck changed. Bravo Company was ambushed by a large contingent of rebels as they were approaching a village and received heavy automatic fire from three sides. Men dropped everywhere with cries of "Medic!". Howard left his cover and darted over to one of the casualties. The man had been struck in the head by a bullet and was dead. Howard rushed to the next casualty. Bullets whizzed all around him like angry bees defending their hive. This man was wounded. Howard applied a field dressing, administered morphine, marked an 'M' on the man's forehead indicating to medical personnel that he had received morphine. Howard dragged the man to cover and continued administering aid to the wounded without regard for his own safety. He lost count of the number of casualties he helped. As Howard dragged another casualty to cover, a rocket-propelled grenade exploded near them. Howard was thrown back by the force of the blast and struck by shrapnel. He tried to crawl to safety but lost consciousness.

Sometime later, Howard sensed being carried on a stretcher. At a field hospital he was triaged, new dressings were applied, and in his semi-conscious state, awaited transport to the U.S. Army Hospital in Landstuhl, Germany. He sensed being carried onto a large aircraft but then lapsed into sleep.

When Howard next woke, he was in a hospital, coming out of surgery. He was aware of pain in his left shoulder and thigh.

The Army notified Clara that Howard had been wounded and was taken to the U.S. Army Hospital in Landstuhl, Germany. He would recuperate there.

Cathy's letter caught up with Howard the week after his surgery.

The news that Clara was in hospice care and Frank was in prison was depressing. *Mom is dying and neither Frank nor I can be with her.*

After several weeks Howard was able to use his left arm and hobble around the ward with a crutch. More weeks of healing and physical therapy followed. At times he thought of the battle in which he was wounded. *I wonder what happened to those guys I helped. I hope some of them make it home.*

19

Hartford, Connecticut, February 2011

At the prison, a guard told Frank, "There's a phone call for you."

The call was from one of the sisters at the hospice.

"Mr. Frazer, I'm calling to tell you that your mother died peacefully last night."

Tears came to Frank's eyes. "Thank you for calling, Sister. As you know, I'm in prison. Is it possible somehow that a funeral can be arranged?"

"We can arrange something," the sister said.

Frank phoned his lawyer, explaining the situation. He asked Mr. Levine to try and locate Howard. "I need to tell him about our mother," he said.

The next day Mr. Levine returned Frank's call.

"I'm sorry about your mother. Howard is a patient in an army hospital in Germany," Levine said. "He was wounded in Iraq. You should be able to reach him at this phone number."

Using the phone in the warden's office, Frank was able to reach his brother.

"Howard, I'm sorry to have to tell you this, but Mom died last night."

"Did she suffer?" Howard asked.

"I don't think so. The nun told me it was peaceful."

"Well, at least she is not suffering anymore," Howard said.

"The thing is," Frank said, "I'm unable to make funeral arrangements, but the nuns told me they would take care of it. I won't be able to attend."

"Yeah, I know. I know about your accident."

"How badly were you wounded?" Frank asked.

"Not too bad, I'll survive," Howard said.

The doctors felt that even though Howard's wounds were not yet completely healed, he would be able to make a short visit to attend his mother's funeral. He was able to obtain a five-day leave and took a flight back to Connecticut.

The nuns provided a modest service for Clara. Cathy was present together with some of Clara's friends and neighbors.

A man approached Howard and introduced himself.

"My name is Martin Levine. I was Clara's lawyer. I'm sorry about your mother, Howard. She was a nice lady. I also represented your brother Frank at his trial. Could you possibly stop in to my office before you return to duty? I drew up a will for your mother some months ago, and I'd like to go over it with you."

"O.K., I'll be there tomorrow. Can I have your address?"

Levine handed Howard his card.

Cathy came over to Howard and kissed him.

"I'm sorry, Howard. Clara really helped me a while ago. I visited her a few times in the hospice. I think she was comfortable there. The nuns took good care of her and kept her mostly free of pain. She hoped to see you and Frank before she passed."

"I know," Howard said, "but this was the earliest I could get away. My wounds are not completely healed. As for Frank, I guess they don't let prisoners attend funerals."

The service was brief. One of the sisters introduced herself to Howard.

"Your mother's passing was peaceful and without pain," she said.

"Thank you so much, Sister, for caring for her and arranging things," Howard said. "I'd like to pay the expenses."

"I'll let you know about that," she said.

Howard took Cathy for lunch at a restaurant. They ordered sandwiches and coffee.

Cathy gazed at her sandwich, avoiding Howard's eyes.

"I'm ashamed to tell you this, Howard, but last year I ran into Frank at a party. We were both drinking and somehow ended up in the same bed. I don't know how it happened, but it did. I became pregnant. When I told my parents, my father threw me out of the house. Frank denied responsibility at first. Then he demanded that I have an abortion. I had no money for an abortion. I asked Frank for the money, and I had to threaten to tell your mother before he agreed to help me. Then I had to chase him down for it, and he only gave me a part. He was nasty." Cathy raised her eyes from her sandwich and looked at Howard. "Frank is not a nice man. I haven't seen him since then. I wanted you to know about it."

"Jesus, Cathy. I don't know what to say. I guess things like this happen. I have to say I'm not surprised. Frank always tended to escape responsibility for some of his actions. Anyway, I'm sorry. I appreciate your telling me. It wasn't necessary."

Cathy changed the subject.

"What was it like in Iraq? How badly were you wounded?"

"My outfit was ambushed. We took a lot of fire, and many of our guys got hit. Some were KIA. I was lucky, they only had to dig some shrapnel out of my shoulder and leg."

Cathy rose. "I've got to go. Take care of yourself, Howard."

She bent, kissed him on the cheek, and rushed off before he could even say goodbye.

Howard sat at the table for a few minutes longer, staring at her uneaten sandwich. *How could Frank do those things? Sleep with Cathy, my former girlfriend? And then treat her that way? What kind of a man has he become?*

The next day, Howard sat in Martin Levine's office. The lawyer read Clara's will to him.

"There was only a small amount of money, about $42,000 and the house. The money is to be divided between you and Frank.

You'll each get about $20,000, after all the fees are paid. She left the house to Frank."

"He was always her favorite," Howard said. "I guess she felt I wouldn't need it, being in the army. What can you tell me about Frank's accident?"

"Well, he got drunk one night, drove at high speed through the city, and crashed into a wooden garbage bin. Unfortunately, a five-year-old child, Emily Cordova, was in the bin at the time and was killed. Frank didn't know about it until the next day."

"What was the little girl doing in the bin?"

"She was searching for her doll that her mother discarded. When I read the police report, I was surprised to see that Frank claimed that you were driving the car. When I asked him about this, he told me that he was frightened and used your name just to gain some time. He knew you were away in the army, and the police couldn't bother you."

Howard sat in silence for a moment or two. *My brother killed a little girl and tried to put the blame on me. I can't believe it.*

Levine continued his explanation.

"Frank was charged with vehicular homicide, D.U.I., and leaving the scene. I was able to get the homicide charge reduced to involuntary manslaughter. He pleaded guilty and was sentenced to eighteen months in prison and a $5,000 fine."

"When will he be released?"

"Sometime in June 2012," Levine said.

"Tell me, Mr. Levine, how would it be if I gave my share of the money to the child's mother? You know, as a way of indicating how sorry I am about what happened."

"That would not be a good idea. The mother can sue Frank in civil court for damages and could be awarded a large sum, although I don't think she will. Anyway, your proposed gift would muddy the waters. If you agree," the lawyer continued, "I'll deposit your share of the money in a bank account in your name. You won't get much interest, but it will always be there safe for whenever you might want or need it."

Howard thanked Levine and arranged to return to Germany on the next available flight.

On the plane, Howard could not get Frank's reckless behavior out of his mind. He found it hard to believe that his brother would do those things. *When we were kids I tried to guide him, but I guess it didn't take. Frank's affair with Cathy was almost incestuous. And then after he got her pregnant he was inconsiderate in demanding that she have an abortion.* Howard recalled his outrage when the lawyer told him how Frank distorted his story to the police. *Frank actually told them that I drove the car. How could a brother do that?*

Howard felt that although he couldn't bring himself to hate Frank, he loathed the things he did. Now that Clara was gone, Hartford was no longer his home. He decided he never wanted to see his brother again.

20

Walter Reed National Military Medical Center, Bethesda, Maryland, June 2011

After six months in Landstuhl, Germany, Howard's wounds were completely healed, and he was transferred to the new tri-service hospital in Bethesda, Maryland for rehabilitation. He underwent a series of physical therapy sessions and was told that he could become an outpatient.

He rented a room with kitchen privileges in an area close to a Metro station and continued visits to the hospital.

Howard had nightmares and mentioned this to one of the doctors who referred him to an army psychiatrist.

"Tell me about your dreams," the psychiatrist asked.

"It's always the same dream," Howard told him. "I'm in a battle and the soldiers in my company keep getting hit, dropping, one after another, and I can't get to them fast enough."

After several sessions the psychiatrist diagnosed Howard with PTSD, the post-traumatic stress disorder common among soldiers. He offered him medication and continued therapy sessions, but Howard refused. His enlistment would be up in December, and he declined the opportunity to re-enlist. An army career no longer appealed to him. *I've had enough war and killing.* Howard received an honorable discharge and was released from the army.

He was now a civilian again. He hung around Washington for a few weeks, visiting the usual tourist sites and wondering what he should do. This saddened him when he thought about Mei Li and the many places they visited. At one point he remembered J.J., but pushed her out of his mind.

I've got to do something. I need to get a job. A job that has a purpose.

In February, he applied as an EMT with an ambulance company. He was readily accepted based on his medical training and experience.

Howard rode in the ambulance day after day. While occasionally he responded to accidents, heart attacks and strokes, most of his calls involved transporting alcoholics, diabetics, and drug addicts to hospital emergency rooms. Many of these patients elected to use 911 and an ambulance ride to an ER rather than use public transportation or a taxi, and Howard was obliged to transport what he perceived as freeloaders. He felt his training was wasted on these patients. He had been doing this for more than a year and was exasperated. *Transporting impaired addicts and alcoholics to the ER is not what I want to do. This is not the job for me. I have no opportunity to use the medical skills I learned in the army. Maybe I could become a paramedic.*

Howard started the course and after six months prepared to take the examination.

21

Hartford, Connecticut, June 2012

On a warm day in June, Frank was released from prison. During those eighteen months, he had plenty of time to think. One of the things he thought about was Howard. *Where was he now? I know he couldn't visit me in prison, but at least he could have phoned or written. I haven't heard from him in over a year.*

Frank found the house empty when he returned. He phoned Mr. Levine to let him know that he had been released.

"Come to my office when its convenient, and I will review your mother's will with you and let you know where money is available."

Frank called the army and eventually learned Howard had been discharged six months ago from the hospital in Bethesda. They had no knowledge of where he was now. Frank recalled Howard had a cell phone and dialed the number without much hope of reaching him. To his surprise, Howard answered.

"It's Frank," he said. "I just wanted to let you know that I was released from prison today. Where are you? What are you doing?"

"I'm working for an ambulance company here in Washington."

"It's been a long time since we got to see each other," Frank said, "five years. Maybe I could come down for a visit?"

"Don't bother," Howard said. "I don't have the time."

"But . . ." Frank was talking to a dial tone. Howard had hung up.

Frank's hands were shaking. *He sounded angry. I'm going to find him.*

Frank called ambulance companies in Washington and soon found one that employed Howard.

Before he left for Washington, Frank made an appointment to see Mr. Levine. In the office, Levine reviewed Clara's will.

"She left the house and the car to you and half of the money. Howard got the rest of the money. I deposited your money in Webster Bank in an account under your name. There is about $20,000, which you can withdraw in whole or in part whenever you wish. Here is the passbook. Good luck, Frank. Is there anything else I can do for you?"

"Yes, can you tell me where my mother is buried?"

The lawyer gave Frank directions to the small cemetery. In the office there, Frank asked where Clara's grave was located. An employee conducted him to the site and then left him alone.

Frank stood there for a few minutes looking at the turf under which his mother lay. Then he cried out, "I'm so sorry, Ma. I wasn't there when you needed me. I was in prison for killing little Emily." Frank wept, his shoulders shaking with sobs.

After a while he composed himself, dried his tears, and walked away. "Tomorrow I will find Howard. Maybe we could be friends again. That's what mom would want."

He called the credit card company he used before entering prison and was able to revalidate his card. Frank lost no time in finding a flight to Washington where he took a taxi to Howard's ambulance company.

Howard was out on a call so Frank waited for him in the office. Howard returned in an hour, walked in to the office, and was stunned to see his brother waiting for him.

"What the Hell are you doing here?" Howard said.

Frank smiled uncertainly. "I wanted to know how you are doing."

Howard glared at his brother. Frank was taller and thinner. "You don't need to know about me, but I know a lot about you. I know you tried to blame me for when you killed that little girl. I also know that you got Cathy pregnant and how your treated her, you rat bastard!"

The color drained from Frank's face. "I didn't mean to blame you for the accident. I was so scared, I was stalling for time and your name was the first thing that came into my head. And that situation with Cathy just happened. I didn't know you still cared about her. I'm sorry about those things Howard. I shouldn't have done them, but I've changed . . ."

"Yeah, like the Pope becomes a Muslim. Get out of my sight, I never want to see you again."

Tears came into Frank's eyes. "I can't change the past, Howard. There's nothing I can do about those things. I'm sorry about Cathy and for telling the police you drove the car. I'll try to be a better man in the future," Frank said quietly and left. He took the next flight back to Hartford.

22

Frank went to see Mr. Spenser. "I've served my time, Mr. Spenser. I'm ready to get back to work again, if you'll have me."

"How bad was it, the prison?" Spenser said.

"I had a lot of time to dwell on my carelessness. I got to know some of the other prisoners and realized I was just like them. Many denied responsibility for their crimes. I was only thinking of myself without regard for anyone else and took the life of an innocent child. I'll never be able to make up for that, but from now on, I'll try to live my life differently."

Spenser considered Frank for a few moments.

"Thank you for sharing your thoughts with me," Spenser said, I'll be glad to have you back."

"I appreciate your confidence in me by hiring me again," Frank said.

"Just do the good work you were doing," Spenser told him. Frank could not help wondering why Mr. Spenser was so kind to him, but he dared not ask.

Frank enjoyed working again. He spent evenings and weekends straightening up his house. He had the windows cleaned and hired a woman who swept, moped, and dusted every room. In the evenings he tried to watch T.V. but mostly found it to be a wasteland. Once in a while he went to a movie, but usually he read books he borrowed from the library. Weeks and months went by.

One morning a young woman entered his cubicle.

"Hi," she said cheerfully. "You are Mr. Frank Frazer, right?" Frank nodded. "I'm Susan Spenser. My father told me about you, and I wanted to meet you."

Susan Spenser was somewhat shorter than Frank with bright green eyes and blond hair tied in a ponytail.

Frank smiled. "Your father is a kind and generous man."

"He said you were the best computer guy in the company," she continued.

"I'm glad he feels that way. He has certainly been good to me. He gave me a job when I desperately needed one."

"If you're so good with computers, why did you need a job so desperately?"

Frank regarded her. Susan was in her early twenties, he figured, well dressed and attractive.

"I'll tell you what," Frank said. "It's lunch time. Why don't we grab some lunch where we can have some privacy? I know a good pizzeria. Thin crust. I'll try to answer any questions you have."

When they were each enjoying a hot slice, she said,

"Okay, how come you needed a job so desperately?"

"Because I just got out of prison," he said.

Susan's eyes opened wide.

She had recently graduated Barnard College with a major in Art History and minors in Music and Comparative Literature. One of her semesters was spent in Rome and Paris.

"I didn't realize—I didn't know—I didn't mean to," she stammered. "Well, what did you . . . I mean, what were you in for?" she asked.

Frank told her about his drunken episode.

"I killed a little girl," he said and went on to explain how it happened. Frank did not tell her how he tried to blame it on his brother nor did he mention his relationship with Howard's girlfriend or its consequences. He was far too ashamed to talk about those things.

"But you didn't know the little girl was in the garbage bin. You didn't mean to kill her," Susan whispered.

"No, of course not, but I drove drunk, and I'll have her on my conscience for the rest of my life." Susan looked at him with sympathy and understanding. She put her hand on top of his. "I hope you'll be discreet about what I've told you," Frank said. "I wouldn't want it to get around the company."

"Don't worry," she told him.

The next day, Susan stopped in to Frank's cubicle.

"How about taking me to lunch?" she said. "This time I'll buy." Frank laughed. He liked this young woman.

She was intrigued by his candor in telling her about the accident and his prison conviction. *What would my father think if I dated him? He's quite attractive. I think he's a good person.*

After several weeks, Frank went to see his boss.

"Mr. Spenser," he started. "Susan and I have been having lunch together, and I'd like to ask her out with your permission."

Spenser was silent for a few moments. *He's just out of prison where he associated with God only knows what kind of men. I have found him to be an honest and sincere young man . . . Does Susan know he was in prison. . . I could talk to her . . .I can't forbid him to see Susan.*

"Susan is a big girl, and she can do whatever she wants. I trust her decisions. And you, young man, don't need my permission, but I appreciate your asking."

During lunch, Frank asked Susan, "What kind of music do you prefer?"

"I like all kinds. Classical, jazz, and folk."

"There's a good program at Tanglewood this Saturday. We could have a picnic on the lawn. The weather should be good. Would you like to go?"

"I'd love to," she said. "I'll bring some sandwiches, and you can bring something to drink."

"That sounds like fun," Frank said, "I don't have my driver's license back yet."

"No problem, I'll pick you up at your house." Frank gave her the address.

Next day, they drove through the Connecticut countryside, finally joining the Tanglewood traffic. Susan carried a basket. Frank brought a blanket and a bottle of white wine. Finding a spot on the lawn they spread the blanket, and Susan revealed the lunch she brought. Frank was surprised when she produced plates and served him pieces of cold chicken, accompanied by French herbed potato salad and deviled eggs. She handed him two wine glasses. Frank realized he had forgotten to bring a corkscrew. Susan smiled and handed him a Swiss Army knife. They finished with slices of Stilton cheese and fresh pears.

"That was delicious and elegant," Frank said. "Where did you find this gourmet stuff?"

Susan faced him with mock severity.

"I'll have you know, Sir, I prepared every morsel with these two hands. I love to cook."

The musicians took their places on the stage and the audience grew quite. Dusk was falling. The first violinist walked onto the stage and bowed to the applause before sounding his "A", followed in turn by the conductor.

As the concert started, Frank and Susan sat side by side on the blanket. One magnificent performance followed another.

Driving home, Susan said, "What a lovely evening. I really enjoyed the concert. Thanks for thinking of it."

In front of Frank's house, he said, "I'd like to see you again."

"That would be nice. I'd like that."

23

August 2012

Frank and Susan began dating. Although he was only eight months older and she was better educated, they enjoyed each other's company. She liked the compassionate way he treated people and his thoughtfulness with her. He was charmed by her sweetness and vivacity. They went to movies, more concerts, and a ball game. Both were Red Sox fans.

"I'd like to show you my house," he said one evening in December. He took her inside and showed her around.

"It's not bad at all," Susan said. "Just needs some painting and touch ups here and there."

In the master bedroom, he said, "This is where my mother lived. I'd like to live here with you."

She turned to him, and they kissed.

"That sounds like a good arrangement," she said. She put her arms around his neck, and they fell onto the bed.

Their lovemaking was a voyage of discovery, passion, and tenderness intermixed and the sweet sleep that followed. He was in love, and it was clear she reciprocated his feelings.

They decided to marry in June. She brought him home for dinner and announced, "Dad, Frank and I are getting married."

Her father was delighted with the news but not surprised. "That's wonderful," he said. "The son I always wanted. You can call me Dad or George," he told Frank. Frank didn't know how to respond. He had no memories of his own father.

Later, Susan advised, "He'd really like you to call him Dad." And Frank readily agreed. He learned Susan's mother died years ago, when Susan was young.

Frank and Susan moved into his house. They spent some money painting and fixing it up and did much of the work themselves. They were happy and in love.

"I'm going to promote you," Spenser told Frank on one day. "Not because you're marrying my daughter, but because you deserve it, and I need your expertise." Frank would now be a manager.

On their honeymoon, Frank and Susan took a trip to Ireland. They had a wonderful time seeing the sites and meeting the people. Frank was delighted Susan enjoyed herself. He loved to see her eyes light up and to hear her laugh.

24

Washington, D.C., March 2014

Television, radio, and newspapers informed the world about the Ebola pandemic raging in West Africa. Howard watched, listened, and read about the thousands of victims of this disease. He visualized natives in the jungle becoming sick and falling over to lie untended on the ground. He dreamed that he went to West Africa trying to help those people.

Howard wanted to learn more about Ebola and on his next day off, he went to the library and asked the librarian. "Where can I find information on Ebola?"

The woman said, "We have some information here, but you will find a comprehensive collection at the National Library of Medicine. It's located in Bethesda on the campus of the National Institute of Allergy and Infectious Disease."

Howard thanked her and took a taxi to the NIAID campus on Executive Boulevard. Once there, he was directed to the building that housed the National Library of Medicine. A security guard requested identification, which Howard produced before being admitted. Inside he found the main reading room. He told a librarian there that he wanted to learn about Ebola.

The woman's face brightened. "You've come to the right place. We have someone here who is an expert on Ebola." She picked up her phone and in a short time a man came over to her desk. She turned to Howard,

"This gentleman is Doctor Zachary Markoff. Right now, he is our resident expert on Ebola."

"Pleased to meet you," Howard said extending his hand. "I'm Howard Frazer."

"I understand you are interested in learning about Ebola," Markoff said. "Come with me, and I'll try to help you."

Howard followed Markoff to his office, a small comfortable room and sat in soft leather chairs.

"I'd like to learn everything I can about Ebola," Howard told him.

"Are you a physician?" Markoff asked.

"No, I'm a paramedic. I was trained in the army and had some experience in Iraq. Now, I work for an ambulance company here in Washington."

"I'm not either," Markoff said. "My Doctorate is in library science, but I've spent a lot of time learning about Ebola hemorrhagic fever, and I'll tell you what I know. I'll just get my notebook so I can refer to it if necessary. Please call me Zach."

"Okay Zach, can you tell me what is hemorrhagic fever?"

"Hemorrhagic fevers are diseases in which the organism attacks the blood vessels causing hemorrhage, damage to the internal organs resulting in shock and often death. Viruses such as Marburg, Lassa and Yellow Fever cause many of these hemorrhagic fevers. Ebola Hemorrhagic Fever (EHF) is one such disease."

"How did Ebola Hemorrhagic Fever get started?"

"The first cases occurred in 1976 in Nzara, a village in Sudan, Africa. A worker in a cotton mill suddenly developed fever, headache, and chest pain with bleeding from his nose and rectum. He died in a few days. Several days later a coworker become ill with the same symptoms, and he died too. People in nearby villages got sick. All in all, 284 people were infected and 150 of them died. The outbreak ended without any explanation, but several months later in Zambuka, Zaire, one thousand three hundred and thirty miles away from Nzara, there was another outbreak. This time 318 people were infected with the staggeringly high mortality of almost ninety percent. This outbreak ended abruptly like the one in Sudan."

"Wow," Howard said, "that's incredible. How did they find out that these outbreaks were caused by the Ebola virus?"

"That's an interesting story. It turns out that a nun who was nursing patients in the missionary hospital in Zaire contracted the disease and died. The Belgium doctor sent samples of her blood to a doctor at the Institute of Tropical Medicine in Antwerp, Belgium. This doctor, a young physician who was studying clinical microbiology, tested the blood for known hemorrhagic fever viruses. He tried to neutralize the virus with known antisera, but none of them worked. He examined the specimen with an electron microscope.

'Look,' he said to his colleagues, 'I've never seen a virus like this! It resembles Marburg virus, but longer. We have got to send this specimen to the National Center for Disease Control (CDC) in Atlanta, Georgia. That is one of the few laboratories capable of handling a dangerous hemorrhagic fever virus.'

The CDC confirmed that the virus was indeed a new one and the Belgian team rushed over to Zambuka, Zaire. There, they met with scientists from the CDC and the World Health Organization (WHO). After collecting and reaffirming all of the available information, the group concluded that the disease was indeed a hemorrhagic fever caused by a previously unknown virus.

The group had questions. Where did the virus hide in the jungle? Was it in an animal or perhaps an insect? They wanted to know how to account for the abrupt appearance and disappearance of human infections. They also wanted to learn how humans become infected. The group considered what to name the virus. One of the doctors suggested Zambuka virus, but another scientist pointed out it would give the village a bad name. In the end they named the virus "Ebola", for the Ebola River in Sudan, where the first outbreak occurred."

"That's very interesting," Howard said.

"The funny thing is," Zachary said, "this outbreak ended like the first one. But over the years, there have been similar outbreaks in Africa. In 1989, Ebola virus came into the United States. Technicians in Reston, Virginia were working with monkeys imported from the Philippines became infected with the virus but did not get sick."

"If they didn't get sick," Howard asked, "how did the doctors know they were infected?"

"Good question. The technicians' blood showed they had developed antibodies against the Ebola virus. By this time, it was obvious that there were a number of subtypes of Ebola virus, and these subtypes varied in virulence causing infections with mortalities ranging from zero to almost ninety percent.

The present Ebola epidemic in West Africa is the largest in history involving several countries, Liberia, Sierra Leone and Guinea. The causative agent is Ebola subtype Zaire, which has a mortality of about fifty percent. There have been 5,600 cases with 2,800 deaths in Liberia alone."

My God! That's more than the numbers of casualties and deaths in the year I was in Iraq.

"Where does Ebola come from, and how do people become infected?"

"It looks like monkeys may carry Ebola, and people coming into contact with them could become infected, but most of the victims never touched a monkey. Close contact with a sick individual, especially any of his body fluids, can transfer the infection."

"Are there any drugs to treat Ebola infections?"

Zachary shook his head. "Unfortunately there is no cure for Ebola, and there is nothing to prevent infection."

"I really appreciate your time and the information," Howard said. "It's a terrible disease."

"It was a pleasure talking with you, Howard. At least you don't have to worry about picking up Ebola patients here," he said in a parting jest.

Over the next few weeks, Howard continued to think about the Ebola epidemic. He couldn't get it out of his mind. *I'm a medic-I wish there was someway I could help those people.*

Each working day, Howard took the Metro for a short ride to the ambulance company where he worked as a paramedic. One evening as Howard was taking the Metro home, a drunken man entered the car. The drunk stood in front of a woman passenger and started to assault her, grabbing at her. The frightened woman attempted to get away. Howard jumped from his seat, grabbed the attacker, and threw him to the floor of the car. Another passenger pushed the emergency button, and the train jolted to a stop. The attacker struggled to get up, but Howard held him down until the police arrived. One of the police officers cuffed the attacker and led him away while another officer questioned the woman and Howard before leaving with the culprit.

The woman appeared shaken. "Let me buy you a cup of coffee," Howard offered. The woman agreed, and they found a small café in the Metro Station.

"What's your name?" he asked.

"My name is Lorraine Benoit. I don't know how to thank you, Mister . . ."

"Frazer," Howard told her. "Please call me Howard."

He thought she was in her early forties. She spoke with a French accent.

"You were very brave, Howard, to come to my rescue."

Howard found himself blushing.

"Do you work here in Washington?" she asked.

"Yes, I'm a paramedic. I work for an ambulance company here in Washington. What do you do?" Howard asked.

"I work for *Medecins Sans Frontieres,*" she explained. "That's Doctors Without Borders. Right now we are desperately trying to cope with a disastrous Ebola epidemic in West Africa."

"I know about the epidemic," Howard said. "I recently learned about it at the National Library of Medicine here in Washington. It's terrible. I wish I could help."

"We could use a man like you." Lorraine went on to tell Howard of the thousands of cases of this dread disease. "You could help make a difference," she told him.

For the first time it struck Howard that he could really go to West Africa and help. *That's what I want to do! I could be a combat medic again.*

25

Howard visited Doctors Without Borders at their office on Virginia Avenue. He told them he wanted to go to West Africa. At the office, a secretary handed him a document listing the requirements for volunteers. These included two years of relevant professional experience, a commitment of a minimum of nine to twelve months, relevant travel and work outside of the U.S., experience as a trainer, computer skills, flexibility, adaptability, and a foreign language, preferably French.

My army training and experience plus the two years as a medic here in D.C. should count. The nine to twelve months is no problem; I have all the time in the world. I guess my trip to Iraq takes care of the travel requirement. I've done some training. I have computer skills. I'm flexible and adaptable. The last one is a problem. I took two years of French in high school, but I can't speak French. Let's see what they say.

Howard completed the application form. A young woman interviewed him. She was impressed with his experience as a combat medic in Iraq.

"Can you document this experience?" she asked.

"Sure, I can get a record from the army. It might take some time."

"Too bad you don't speak French, but we really need people now, especially in Liberia," she said. "When would you be ready to go?"

"I can go this afternoon," Howard said with a smile.

The woman laughed. "Do you have a telephone contact?"

Howard gave her his cell phone number.

"We'll call and let you know. Good luck."

The call came the next day. They would take him! He was told to return to the office for travel information. He went to a travel center, had photos taken, and was able to obtain a passport the following day. He called the ambulance company and told them he had decided to go to West Africa and help fight Ebola. As directed, Howard took the train to New York and a taxi to JFK where he waited to board Air France flight KL6140 to Brussels. En route, he reviewed some of the material given to him at the Doctors Without Borders' office.

Howard read, *in 1968, a group of young doctors in Paris decided to help victims of wars and major disasters. They were to become the* Medecins Sans Frontieres *or MSF. By 1971, MSF was officially created with 300 volunteers. Their fundamental belief was that all people have the right to medical care regardless of gender, race, religion, creed, or political affiliation. Since it's founding, MSF has treated more than a hundred million patients. Almost all of their support comes from private donors.*

In Brussels, the immigration officer checked Howard's passport and directed him to a woman who waited there. She wore a jacket with "MSF" on the front.

"Monsieur Frazer?" she asked.

"Yes, that's me, but I don't speak French."

"That's too bad," she said. "Please come with me."

Howard followed her to a small office in the terminal building with "MSF" on the door. Inside, a nurse greeted him.

"We're glad you are here, Mr. Frazer. Please remove your jacket and roll up your sleeves. We need to give you some immunizing injections."

Howard complied by rolling up his shirtsleeves. "What kind of injections?"

"Typhoid, yellow fever, hepatitis A, tetanus booster, and flu," she told him. "Your arms will be sore for a day or so." She handed him a bottle of pills. "These are for malaria, take one today and one every week while you are in West Africa. Continue for a few weeks after you leave. Also, here's some mosquito repellent. While you are there, put it on if you go out in the evening or in the countryside."

The woman who brought Howard to the office asked, "Would you like some coffee and a biscuit?"

Howard thanked her. "No, I'm going to look around the terminal for a while."

"We have a cot here you can use while waiting for your flight," she told him. "The office is open around the clock."

The next day Howard boarded a Belgian flight to Casablanca with one stop in Dakar where there was a nine and a half hour layover. The final leg was to Roberts International Airport in Monrovia, the capital of Liberia.

Walking from the aircraft through a warm rain, he entered the terminal. The building showed evidence of war. There were numerous bullet holes in the walls and portions of the roof were destroyed. Many soldiers in grey-green camos walked around, some carrying rifles.

Howard was exhausted. He picked up his knapsack and carryall and looked around to see if someone had been sent to meet him.

26

Liberia, West Africa, April 2014

A white man approached Howard. "Are you Howard Frazer?" Howard nodded.

"I'm Rory Donnelly," he said, extending his hand. "Here to pick you up."

"British?" Howard asked.

"Australian," he said with a grin. Rory wore khaki shorts and a short-sleeved shirt. He looked to be about the same age as Howard. He led Howard to a Jeep fitted with a cover. Howard flung his knapsack and carryall in the back and climbed aboard.

"What troops are those in the terminal?" Howard asked. "I didn't recognize the uniform."

"They are U.N. peacekeepers, we have five thousand of them in uniform. We need them. There have been two civil wars here in Liberia and some border incidents."

"How long has it been raining?" Howard asked, as they got started.

Rory laughed. "Better get used to it, Mate. This is the rainy season."

"How long does it last?"

"It runs from April to October. Monrovia is the wettest capital in the world. It even rains a little in the dry season."

"How far is Monrovia?"

"About 37 miles."

As they grew closer to the city, Howard observed evidence of extreme poverty. He saw a man squatting to defecate in the street.

"Is that common?" he asked Rory, calling attention to the defecator.

"Unfortunately, it is. Only about one third of the population have toilets, and the sewage system is primitive at best."

"What can you tell me about Ebola? I've had some medical training."

"Medical school?" Rory asked.

"No, I was a U.S. Army combat medic in Iraq. My training was something like a paramedic."

"I'm pretty much the same, Mate. I can tell you Ebola is one of the hemorrhagic fevers, caused by an unusual RNA virus. We don't know what the reservoir is, but it's a killer. Mortality here runs about 50 percent. The virus damages the inside of blood vessels causing hemorrhages over the entire body."

"How does it first show up in the victims?" Howard asked.

"There is an incubation period of about two weeks following infection, but it can be as short as two days. The first signs and symptoms of Ebola are sudden. It starts with high fever, headache, fatigue, vomiting, and diarrhea. Or it could start with a cough. Some of the patients develop a rash after a few days. The diarrhea becomes watery with abdominal cramps. This severe fluid loss leads to dehydration, electrolyte imbalance, hypotension, and shock."

"How did this epidemic get started?" Howard asked.

"Beats me. I've heard the first cases of Ebola were in Guinea last year, but it spread like wildfire into

Sierra Leone and Liberia. It is the largest epidemic of Ebola in history. Here in Liberia, there have been about 5,600 cases with 2,800 deaths. Cases are doubling every 15-20 days."

"How do you treat it?"

"There is no vaccine or any specific treatment. What we do is supportive—control dehydration with oral fluids when possible, try to maintain electrolyte balance and blood pressure."

"How did the disease spread so fast?" Howard asked.

"The virus is present in every human body fluid—tears, saliva, mother's milk, blood, urine, vaginal fluid, semen, and feces. If any of these fluids reaches even the slightest break in the skin, infection is sure to follow. We have to work wearing personal protective equipment, PPE."

As they entered the city Rory said, "This section is known as Sinkor." They pulled up in front of a large tent. "Here is where we are billeted." Inside Howard saw many cots, each with mosquito netting. "Pick any bed not being used," Rory told him, "but always get under the mosquito netting even if you're just lying down to rest. Malaria is rampant here, and many of our patients have malaria as well as Ebola. Do you have meds for malaria?"

"Yes. The nurse at MSF gave me a bottle of them."

"Don't forget to take them, Mate," Rory said.

Howard threw his gear on one of the beds.

"Let's go, Mate. Got to get to work." Howard accompanied Rory to another large tent.

"You've got to learn how to use your PPE," Rory told him. One of the nurses showed Howard how to put on the gown, mask, head covering, apron, booties, and gloves. She did not speak much English, but she managed to explain to Howard that in this warm climate, work in the PPE was limited to about one hour.

Next, Rory turned Howard over to one of the charge nurses. "I've got to go," he said. "She'll show you what to do. I'll see you around. Good luck."

27

This nurse took Howard to another large tent. Inside, he could see the entire area was filled with cots so closely packed with barely enough space for the nursing staff to move between them. The cots were filled with patients, most of whom lay motionless. Howard heard low moans, groans, and cries. He was nearly overcome by the odors of excrement and vomit.

The charge nurse stationed Howard at the door of the tent.

"We are completely filled," she explained. "You will start by doing triage. You need to explain to these poor people we cannot help them, and they must go home. They all understand English." She turned and walked away leaving Howard to face the line of black faces pleading to be admitted. He started to sweat in his PPE.

The people were in all stages of illness. Some of them had just become sick, while others looked to be dying. Howard was filled with pity for these people. Each in turn begged Howard to be admitted or at least to have their sick companion treated.

"Please Sir, it's my wife. She's very sick."

"Please Sir, you've got to help us, my brother is awful sick."

"I'm begging you Sir, my mother is so sick, and I can't help her anymore."

Howard was overwhelmed as he turned each petitioner away. With tears in his eyes he told them there were no more beds available. He issued gloves and masks to those carrying a sick relative and explained the importance of avoiding physical contact with the sick person. After an hour, Howard couldn't take it any longer. As if expecting his imminent collapse, the charge nurse reappeared with another worker to relieve Howard. She led him away so he could divest himself of the PPE, drink some water, and rest for a while. Later, Howard was assigned to explain to other groups of people how to isolate and care for an Ebola patient.

By the end of the day, Howard was exhausted. He entered the mess tent for MSF workers, found some rations, and ate them.

He staggered to his tent, flopped on his bed, attached the mosquito netting and slept.

28

Monrovia, July 2014

Day followed day for Howard. Each was the same, several shifts of triage at the hospital door and the rest of the time teaching Ebola victims how to isolate sick people and to avoid personal contact.

The horrors he experienced were far greater than those he encountered in Iraq. Here, there seemed to be no end of the continual death and dying. Rory Donnelly was no longer there. Howard learned he had been assigned to another location.

After two months, one of the charge nurses told Howard, "The number of cases up at Kaba Town has increased, and we could use more help there. Do you think you're ready to start patient care?" she asked.

"That's what I came here for," Howard said. "I'm ready." An MSF worker drove Howard to the new location. It was one of the northern sections on the outskirts of the city. Howard was glad to see Rory, a friendly face. Rory introduced Howard to the staff.

One of the charge nurses was Jeanne Mallette. She was a handsome woman, in her late 30's with gray eyes that seemed to reflect sorrow.

"I'm glad to meet you, Howard," she said, looking him over as if to assess his capability. "We can certainly use another pair of hands." When Jeanne, Rory and Howard sat together for a brief meal, Howard observed Jeanne seldom smiled.

Later, Rory told Howard that Jeanne had been engaged to one of the MSF doctors. The previous week, she learned her fiancé had been killed on an MSF assignment in the Central African Republic. When Howard tried to console her for her loss she told him, "He died doing the work he loved. The only thing I can do is to continue our work."

Jeanne spent time to make certain Howard used his PPE correctly. She also checked on the various procedures Howard performed to ensure he did them properly.

"Why all this special attention?" Howard asked. "I've already been trained in these techniques."

"You are new here, Howard, and I want to make sure you do everything right for your protection and for our patients." She smiled briefly. "But I see you know them all perfectly."

Jeanne liked talking with Howard and Rory. They developed a close relationship, both friendly and professional. The three continued to spend time together whenever they had a few moments in the heavy work schedule.

Medicines and other materials, including beds, were in short supply. The three of them worked long hours each day trying to keep up with the growing patient load. Each time one of the patients died, Jeanne considered it a personal loss and mourned. Howard wondered what steps could be taken to stem the epidemic. Burial rites of the natives involved close contact with the body of the deceased during which the family members also became infected. This practice added to the number of cases.

One evening, after a hectic day, Howard joined Rory and Jeanne in the mess tent for supper. They were all exhausted when Rory excused himself saying, "Be back in a minute."

Rory returned carrying his guitar. He sat down and started to strum a few quiet chords. The music had a relaxing quality, and several other staff workers came over to join them. Rory started to sing quietly, songs he remembered. He was an Irish tenor, and his clear voice evoked smiles and a few chuckles with *Meg Flaherty's Drake* and *The Maid Of The Sweet Brown Knowe.* One of the staff members, an Englishman, remarked, "It's nice to have a bit of music amidst all this disease and death."

Towards the end of October, American troops arrived, nearly 3,000 of them including the 36th Engineering Brigade and elements of the 101st Airborne. The Americans set out to do what they were good at—building. They constructed wooden Ebola Treatment Units in Monrovia and the surrounding countryside. Each ETU was designed for triage, together with four giant tents for patients, referred to as the "hot zone." They also provided large quantities of medicines and medical supplies. Cases started to decline a few weeks later, but no one had any explanation for the decrease.

"What on earth impelled the U.S. to send all this aid to Liberia rather than other stricken countries in West Africa, like Sierra Leone and Guinea?" Howard asked Rory.

"It's an interesting story," Rory told him. "I'll tell you what I've heard. It seems like four years ago, Ellen Johnson-Sirleaf, the president here, contacted your President Obama. He invited her to the White House. As a result, he built the 25-bed hospital in Monrovia to care for MSF workers who caught Ebola. This, of course, was just a drop in the bucket, as you Yanks say. Then, a few weeks ago, she wrote telling him about the thousands of cases of Ebola threatening to overwhelm the country unless significant aid occurred."

"And all this help, all these troops, were Obama's response to the letter?" Howard asked.

"Well, remember your President is himself an Afro-American. Obama must have remembered how Liberia got started. It appears that a few years before your Civil War, there were thousands of free Negroes living in the States. Their masters had freed some, and others were the children of those freed slaves. These Negroes were not citizens. They had no rights and were shunned by the whites, who considered them to be an ignorant and dangerous group. One of your Congressmen got the idea to ship them all here to Liberia. Most of these Negroes considered themselves Americans and did not want to go, but eventually a few hundred agreed to come here, and your Congress appropriated some money. The idea proved to be a disaster. The native Africans here regarded these black Americans with hostility and over the years there were two civil wars, but eventually President Sirleaf, apparently a savvy woman, got things organized, and the country did well until Ebola struck."

"That's interesting. It's news to me," Howard said. "They didn't teach it in our history class, but I guess Obama recognized our country owed something to Liberia."

On a Sunday morning in December, Howard woke feeling feverish. His head ached, and he had pain in his chest and abdomen. He tried to sit up but fell back with a groan. Rory, who slept close to Howard asked, "What's up, Mate?"

"I feel sick," Howard groaned. Rory walked over and felt Howard's forehead. "You're burning up," he said. "I'll get Jeanne."

A few minutes later, Rory returned with Jeanne who took Howard's temperature. It was 104.2. She noted a rash over his face and chest.

"*Mon Dieu*," she said. "You got it, *Cherie*. Stay there, we'll be right back." She addressed the other volunteers who slept in the tent. "Don't anyone touch him!"

Jeanne and Rory returned wearing their PPE gear. "We're moving you to a clean bed in the hospital tent," she told Howard.

Rory helped Howard to get up and to walk to the hospital tent. Howard was extremely weak. They found a clean bed for him and pulled the mosquito netting over him.

"Don't worry, Howard. We'll take care of you," Jeanne said.

Howard lay there in pain. *I'm going to die.* He developed a cough and diarrhea. Jeanne and Rory visited him often, giving him medicines and water. The next day Howard started to bleed. He bled from his eyes, his nose, his mouth, and his urine contained blood.

"This hemorrhaging is not in itself life threatening," Jeanne told Rory. "It just shows the terrible damage the virus is doing to his blood vessels and organs."

Howard became sicker and despite efforts to get him to drink water, he became dehydrated and lapsed into episodes of unconsciousness. As he lay there, fragments of memory flashed through his mind. He dreamed of being in a battle in Iraq. Many members of his company fell, dead or wounded. Howard rushed over to each, trying to save them. Many were black and suffered from Ebola. Howard recognized his brother Frank was one of the wounded. Frank was dying despite Howard's efforts to save him. He experienced great pity for his brother. He forgave Frank for trying to blame him for killing the little girl and for getting Cathy pregnant.

Jeanne became his personal nurse despite her other duties. She managed to obtain an IV set and administered fluid to Howard. His blood pressure decreased.

"We're losing him," Jeanne cried and increased her efforts to save him. In his confusion, Howard imagined it was Mei Li who was caring for him.

29

Monrovia, December 2014

Howard lingered for two weeks and then gradually improved. By the end of the third week he was conscious, but had lost thirty pounds and was extremely weak.

"Where is Jeanne?" he asked Rory.

Rory shook his head. "I'm sorry to tell you this, Mate, but she's gone. She caught Ebola and died last night."

"Oh, my God," Howard said. "Why? Didn't she take precautions? Wear her PPE?"

"Of course she did. She was an experienced nurse."

Tears came to Howard's eyes. "She could have caught it nursing me," he said.

Howard took the news of Jeanne's death hard. *It looks like bad things happen to women I liked or loved. Cathy got pregnant, Mei Li left me to marry someone in China, and now Jeanne dies taking care of me. I hope J.J. is O.K.* Howard became depressed and lost interest in the work.

"Look, Mate," Rory said to him one evening. "She could have gotten it from anyone. Don't take it personally. We've got to get you out of here to someplace where you can get proper care. I guess you'd like to go back to the States."

"No there's nothing for me back there. I've got no family left," Howard said. "Right now I don't know where I should go, and I don't much give a damn."

"Tell you what, Mate. I've about had it here. Cases are decreasing, and I want to go home, back to Australia. Why don't you come home with me? We could get you fixed up and then have a good life. What do you say?"

"Why not?" Howard said with a shrug.

Howard was declared cured, no longer infective, and was discharged from the hospital tent. Rory helped him back to his quarters and brought him food everyday although Howard had little appetite.

After several weeks, Howard gradually became stronger and regained some of the weight he lost. Eventually Rory came to him and said, "We're all set, Mate. I reserved our flight. We're leaving next week."

As their aircraft took off, Howard's view of Liberia receded and then disappeared as their plane entered a cloud layer. Howard's mind raced. *Goodbye Africa. I spent eight months in that place trying to help those poor people deal with that horrible disease. At first I pitied them, but then I came to respect and admire their determination and courage. Many had little or nothing, and they had to endure watching family and friends die all around them. I wonder how I would do in the face of such adversity. At least the number of cases is decreasing, although we don't know why. We must find a vaccine and a cure for Ebola, but I'm through with Ebola.* But Ebola was not yet finished with Howard.

The flight from Monrovia to Dubai, in the United Arab Emirates, was a long one. Howard and Rory sat in the terminal for many hours admiring the modern, spotless facility.

"Tell me about your family?" Howard asked.

"Well, first of all, there are my parents, John and Maureen Donnelly. Then, there is my older brother Jack and my younger sister Ellen. Then there is Millie. She lives with us. She's not family, but she's been with us a long time, helps my mother with the housework."

"And where did you say you lived?"

"We live on our farm in a town called Warren. We're in the north part of New South Wales, near the MacQuarry River."

"What's it like there?" Howard asked.

"Well, we have 1,600 acres of land. We grow cotton in the summer and wheat in the winter."

"What's the social life like?"

Rory laughed. "It's somewhat better than Liberia. There's a movie house in town, and that's about it."

"How do you meet friends, you know, girls? Do you have a girlfriend?"

Rory's expression became serious. "No."

"How come?" Howard persisted.

"I thought you might know, Howard. I'm a Puff."

"I don't understand. Is it something like the Magic Dragon?"

Rory did not smile. "I'm gay, Howard." The men sat in silence for a moment.

"What's the problem?" Howard asked.

"No problem with me. My family knows, and they accept me. Do you have a problem with it?"

"Hell no," Howard said. "I'm not going to tell you some of my best friends are gay, because it's not true. I never knew anyone who was gay. You've been a good friend to me, and I don't care. Can't we just stay friends?"

"You bet your ass," Rory said. "Whoops, I didn't mean . . ." Both men roared with laughter.

30

Hartford, Connecticut June 2014

Frank and Susan vacationed in Italy the following year. They toured Rome, museums in Florence, went to an opera in Milan, reveling in Italian food and wines.

On their return, Susan discovered she was pregnant. She went to see her doctor for a prenatal examination.

"You're fine," her doctor told her. "The only thing is your blood pressure is slightly higher than normal. I don't want to give you any medication, just try to limit your salt intake." Susan agreed to try. She loved potato chips, pretzels, and other salty snacks.

Both expectant parents were overjoyed and spent time fixing up one of the rooms to be a nursery. They purchased a crib and a ton of baby clothes, diapers, bottles, and a variety of paraphernalia American babies require. Susan and Frank attended classes on birthing and nursing. An ultrasound indicated their baby was a girl and pink became the predominant color in the nursery. They decided to call her Melissa.

In the evenings, they would sit together and talk about Melissa.

"She'll be great in kindergarten," Susan said.

"Yes, she'll be a wiz in grade school," Frank said.

"And in high school," they both chorused.

"Should we send her to a private school?" Frank asked.

Two days before her due date, Susan felt contractions. That night she was awakened by severe abdominal cramps and back pain. She woke Frank, gasping, "I'm bleeding, a lot." Vaginal blood was rapidly saturating her underwear.

Frank became alarmed.

"I don't think this is normal," he said. "Let's get you to the hospital right away." It was 2:00 a.m.

At the hospital emergency room, Frank rushed in and yelled, "My wife's bleeding—a lot! She's having a baby."

Two nurses ran out, put her on a gurney, and rushed her into the ER. A doctor made a quick examination. "She needs to go to the operating room right now!" he shouted.

Susan was rushed to the OR. Frank ran along side trying to hold her hand.

"It'll be okay, Honey," she said. They wheeled her into the OR. Frank had to remain in the corridor.

It will be okay, he told himself. *This is a good hospital. They will take care of her.*

Frank heard the page "Code Blue, second floor OR."

A doctor wearing scrubs rushed in to the operating room. Frank was scared. After a few minutes, a nurse ran from the operating room down the hall. Minutes later she reappeared with another nurse, carrying bags of blood.

Frank panicked. *What's happening? Why do they need all that blood?* During the next hour and a half Frank paced back and forth, his mind in torment. *Please, God, don't let her die. I can't call Dad until I know what's happening.*

A doctor emerged from the operating room and approached Frank. His scrubs were covered with blood, and his face was grave. "Mr. Frazer . . ."

"What's wrong?" Frank asked. "Tell me!"

"I'm terribly sorry," the doctor said. "We've lost her. We couldn't stop the bleeding. The placenta had torn away from the uterus. We tried a crash C-section but . . ."

"You mean she's dead?"

The doctor nodded.

"The baby?" Frank asked. "My little girl? My Melissa?"

"There was no heartbeat when your wife arrived."

"How could this happen?" Frank demanded.

"It's called placental abruption. We don't know why, but sometimes the placenta tears off from the uterus tearing the connecting blood vessels. This deprives the baby of its blood supply. It's a rare event, and there's no way you could have known. Did your wife have any trauma to her abdomen?"

"No, nothing. She was fine."

"I'm so sorry," the doctor said, then turned and with slumped shoulders walked back into the operating room.

Frank was in shock.

"No!" He cried. *This is my punishment for killing little Emily.* He sat down and wept uncontrollably. After awhile a nurse came and offered him some coffee. Frank turned on his cell phone and called his father-in-law. It was 4:30 am. "Dad," he croaked, "Susan had a sudden hemorrhage. I rushed her to the hospital, but they couldn't do anything. They're both gone, Susan and Melissa." Frank was sobbing.

Frank went home to the empty house. It was still dark. He remained in the house alone. If he took food, he did not remember. He slept in his clothes and did not wash or shave. He was overcome with feelings of guilt. He kept repeating, "It's my punishment, it's my punishment." The phone rang, but he did not answer it.

The next day the doorbell rang. Frank opened the door to stare blankly at his father-in-law. Spenser's face was haggard, and his eyes were red from weeping.

"Can I come in?" George said. "You look terrible. When was the last time you had something to eat?"

Frank stepped aside to let him enter.

"I don't know," he said.

"I'll wait while you take a hot shower and shave," George told him. "Then I want you to come with me. We have to arrange for Susan and the baby."

The small funeral took place in the Congregational Church. There were two caskets. Frank wept unabashedly during the service. A few friends and employees were present. At the cemetery, Frank and his father-in-law watched, weeping as the two coffins were lowered into the ground.

Afterward, George turned to Frank, "Let's get some hot food."

"Dad, I don't feel like . . ."

"No, we have to talk."

After they had eaten, George asked, "What will you do now, Frank?"

"I don't know, Dad. I just don't know."

"Listen Frank, I'm too old to marry again and have another daughter for you, but life must go on. You have to find something to do."

"I want to stay with you, Dad. If you still want me."

"You need to go back to work," George told him. "We both must. It's what Susan would have wanted us to do. And I don't know if I can manage without you."

31

Sydney, New South Wales, Australia, January 2015

The flight to Sydney was a long one. After clearing customs and immigration, Rory phoned his family to say he had arrived in Sydney. The men found a taxi to take them to a different part of the airport.

"Where are we going?" Howard asked.

"We need to get an air taxi to fly us to Dubbo."

"I don't understand. Why can't someone pick us up here in Sydney?"

Rory laughed. "Warren is about seven hours by car from Sydney. Dubbo is the nearest airport to Warren. We do have a small air strip in Warren, but it's private and just used for crop dusting."

The men found a pilot with an air taxi company who was willing to fly them to Dubbo in his small airplane. Rory's brother waited there with a pickup truck. The brothers embraced, slapping each other on the back. Rory introduced Howard when he was able to extricate himself from his brother's hug. "This is Jack."

"Glad to know you, Howard. Welcome to Australia," Jack said.

The men climbed into the truck and started off. Howard was surprised to see the steering wheel on the right side of the truck. He sat where the driver normally sat and winced as another car approached, anticipating a collision.

"Not to worry, Mate. We Aussies drive on the proper side of the road," Jack said.

For the next hour and a half, Howard gazed at the countryside and listened to Jack relate the family news. It was hot and dusty. The land was flat with few trees. Flies and other insects spattered the windshield. At last, the truck pulled up in front of a farmhouse.

"This is it," Jack said.

Rory leaped out of the truck and ran toward the house where his parents waited on the porch. His father, a lean, balding man with a wide smile, shook Rory's hand. "Glad to have you home, Lad."

Rory turned to introduce Howard. "This is my father."

"Call me John," the father said. "You're welcome here."

Rory's mother, a thin woman, with streaks of gray in her hair, embraced Rory. "Welcome home, Son." She turned to Howard. "I'm Maureen, Rory's Mum. Rory wrote us all about you," she said. "You're welcome to stay with us as long as you wish. Consider yourself a member of the family. Come inside."

Jack parked the truck and joined them to enter a large room lit by daylight. A long dinner table occupied the center of the room. In back, Howard could see a flight of stairs leading to an upper floor. He also noticed a spinet. "I see you have a piano," Howard observed.

"Yes," John told him. "We're a musical family, except for me. Maureen is an accomplished pianist, and Rory plays the guitar. He, Jack, and Ellen all have good voices."

"Where's Ellen?" Rory asked.

As if on cue, a young woman in her late 20's burst in, threw herself at Rory hugging him fiercely. "It's so good to see you Rory! You're looking well. How was Africa?"

"It was awful," he said laughing and made a motion as if to swat her behind which she ducked.

"This is my sister, Ellen," he said to Howard.

Ellen offered Howard a firm handshake. "Nice to meet you, Howard." She was nearly as tall as he, slim, with wide set blue eyes, a pert nose, and an engaging smile. Her brown hair was tied in a ponytail.

"You just have time to wash up before dinner," Maureen told the new arrivals. "Rory will show you your room, Howard."

Howard's room was small, but comfortably furnished. Through a window, he could see the flat land stretching white far into the distance. *That must be cotton*. His room shared a bathroom with Rory's bedroom. Howard washed the dust from his hands and face and used his fingers to comb his hair. He could smell good food cooking.

Dinner was a rich lamb stew served by a short, rotund woman who smiled at Rory and Howard.

"This is Millie," Maureen said to Howard, by way of introduction.

"You're the first American I've met," Millie responded. "Nice to meet you, Howard."

"Hi," Howard said with a smile.

"Well, now you can see Americans don't have horns and a tail," Jack teased. Everyone laughed.

"Years ago," Maureen explained, "I was looking for someone to help with the housework. I went to an employment agency. While I waited to talk to an agent, I found myself sitting next to Millie. She told me her name and asked if I had any sprogs at home. I told her I had three plus a large farmhouse, which was getting too big for me to manage alone. 'I want the job' Millie told me. 'I always wanted children, but they never came along,' she added. Millie didn't even ask me what the salary was. I hired her right away, and she's been with us ever since. She cleans, does the washing, and the cooking. She's like a family member. The only thing is, she doesn't put enough salt in the food."

Everyone laughed. "My husband had heart disease," Millie said, "he was on a low salt diet. I took care of him for many years until he died. I guess I got to think of salt as being bad for your health."

After dinner, Howard and the younger Donnellys walked outside and sat on the small front porch.

"That's a lot of cotton out there," Howard said. "It's so thick I don't even see any leaves."

"We had them sprayed a few days ago with a chemical causing the plants to think it's fall and shed their leaves. This makes it much easier for us to pick the cotton," Jack explained. "I'm mighty glad you're home, Rory. We can use another pair of hands around here. Will you be staying long?"

Rory smiled. "I'm done with my traveling for the next fifty years or so," he said. "I'm staying here for awhile."

That night as Howard lay in bed waiting for sleep to come, his thoughts took him back over the past years. *It was so long ago, like a different life. Trying to become a plumber before I enlisted.* His jaw tightened with anger and disgust when he thought of his brother. *How could Frank do those things—trying to blame me for his drunken episode which killed the little girl, and then start fucking my girlfriend, Cathy, knocking her up and forcing her to have an abortion?* He pushed those thoughts from his mind. *I remember basic training, Sergeant Chavez and the boxing lessons, and learning to be a medic at Fort Sam. Then there was J.J. She was a hot one. And sweet Mei Li, I really loved her. It took Iraq to get her out of my mind. Then Liberia*. The last thing he thought before he drifted into sleep was the overwhelming horror of Ebola and the death of Jeanne Mallette.

32

In the weeks that followed, Howard found himself fully accepted into the Donnelly family. Everyone seemed to have something to do except Howard who felt useless. *I'm a non-paying guest here.*

Rory contacted his former employer. The ambulance company was glad to have him back. Ellen resumed her classes in agriculture and business at Warren College. It was time to pick the cotton, and that kept Jack busy supervising the seasonal workers. Maureen and Millie spent hours preparing meals for the workers. John took care of the paper work, keeping track of bills and payments, arranging for the cotton to be processed, bailed, and shipped. Nevertheless, he was able to make time for long conversations with Howard.

Ellen had considerable time off from her classes and offered to show Howard around the countryside. Together they walked into town along the river.

The weather was hot and dry. A small cluster of pepper trees and gum trees around the house provided shade and some relief from the burning sun. Flies were everywhere and a constant nuisance. Other insects, such as grasshoppers, locusts, and spiders were abundant.

In the trees, Howard saw and heard a variety of birds. Ellen pointed out parrots, parakeets, cockatoos, and kookaburras. Out in the country on different days, she showed him a group of emus.

Ellen told him, "These huge flightless birds have eggs the size of footballs."

On another day, they saw a huge troop of kangaroos, hundreds of them.

Howard found Ellen to be charming and knowledgeable. She was energetic, and Howard realized she had a strong love for the land, the farm, and her family. From time to time, she asked Howard about his family, and one day he spoke of his brother Frank.

"Do you have any sibs?" she asked.

"I used to have a brother, but not anymore. We were close when we were kids," Howard told her. "But then he did some things that pissed me off, and I don't see him anymore."

Ellen was curious. "What did he do?"

Howard told her about Frank's drunken episode which resulted in the death of a child. "He tried to blame me for it, can you believe that?" He did not mention anything about Frank and Cathy.

Ellen was sympathetic. She was quiet for a few minutes. She laid her hand on his arm and said, "It's too bad when brothers hate each other." Howard liked the feeling of her hand on his arm. He did not respond.

One afternoon, when Howard and the entire Donnelly family were sitting on the porch, Millie came out to announce, "A package arrived for you, Howard. I'll just go and fetch it."

"How could any mail reach me here?" Howard asked no one in particular.

"I told the MSF people you were coming home with me," Rory said.

" . . . and I gave them my address in Hartford when I volunteered," Howard added.

Millie returned and handed the package to Howard. "It came from the U.S. Department of Defense in Washington."

"Uh oh," Howard said as he opened the package. "I hope they're not trying to get me back in the army."

The package contained two smaller decorative boxes, each with a folded sheet of paper. Howard opened one of the sheets and read.

"What does it say, Howard?" Jack asked.

Howard read aloud, "To Corporal Howard Frazer: You have been awarded the Purple Heart Medal for wounds you received in combat on January 5, 2011, while serving in Iraq." The small box contained the award, a purple heart shaped medal with a white cameo of George Washington on the surface. He held it up so the others could see it. There were exclamations of praise.

"This is no big deal," Howard explained. "Everyone who gets themselves wounded in combat receives one of these." They all laughed.

He unfolded the paper attached to the second box and read aloud, "To Corporal Howard Frazer: The Secretary of the Army has awarded you The Bronze Star Medal for heroic or meritorious service or achievement while engaged in action against an enemy of the United States on January 5, 2011." The medal itself was indeed shaped like a star suspended from a red, white, and blue ribbon. On the face of the medal was inscribed, "For Howard Frazer" and below "For Heroic or Meritorious Service." This time the revelation was greeted with silence.

"Wow!" Rory said.

"I'm impressed," Jack said.

"You're a hero," Ellen said.

Howard was embarrassed. He did not know what to say. "I . . . I . . .didn't know at the time. Maybe they gave it to me by mistake." This time, nobody laughed.

"What was it like over in Iraq?" John asked.

"We had good days and bad days," Howard said. "My unit was tasked to support the Iraqi soldiers, you know, teaching them how to fight. Those were the good days. The Iraqis were friendly and cooperative, but they didn't want to fight. From time to time my company had surprise attacks by the rebels. The last one was bad. We were ambushed and took a lot of casualties."

"Was that when you were wounded?" Ellen asked.

Howard nodded.

April 2015

Howard enjoyed his association with the Donnelly family, but was still concerned that he was a guest. He wanted to find some work and contribute to the family income.

He asked Rory, "Is there something I could do to help with the work on the farm? I need something to do."

Rory laughed. "Sorry, Mate, but all those jobs are filled. Jack oversees the workers, Mom and Millie feed them, Dad and Ellen take care of the paperwork. Why not just relax and enjoy the ride?"

"I can't do that, Rory. Besides, I'd like to pay my way. You know, contribute to the Donnelly income. I don't want to be a freeloader."

"I don't know what to tell you, Mate. I don't work on the farm."

"Yeah, but you contribute from your job. Is there any chance for me to work for your ambulance company? You know I've got all the training and experience."

"I don't know, but I'll check it out. You would probably have to get certified."

After a few days, Rory told Howard, "The chaps and the boss would like to meet you. There is a possibility we could use you."

The next day, Howard accompanied Rory and met his boss, Sandy MacAllister, and the others. After some discussion, Sandy told Howard there was a job for him if he could pass the certification exam and satisfy the training and experience requirements. Howard was enthusiastic and filed an application for the certification. In time, he sat for the exam and described his training and experience in detail. He passed the exam and was certified as a paramedic in Australia.

When Howard first offered a portion of his salary to John Donnelly, he was surprised. "Howard, you don't have to pay us. You are our guest and welcome as long as you want to stay. We consider you a part of our family."

"I appreciate that, John, but if you consider me part of the family then you must permit me to contribute like the other family members."

John took out his pipe, filled it with fragrant tobacco and lit it, considering Howard's offer. John finally accepted his offer and told Howard his contribution would be welcomed.

Howard's work schedule provided time for him to spend with Ellen. Other than his teenage romance with Cathy and his affair with Mei Li, Howard had not had a serious relationship with a woman. His time in the army and in West Africa kept him fully occupied. He felt the hours he spent with Ellen to be precious. He admired her openness, warmth, and sincerity, but had not expressed his tender feelings for her. He wasn't certain how she felt about him.

On a warm afternoon in early May, Howard and Ellen were walking by the river. She hooked her arm through his bringing them closer. He could smell the faint scent of the fragrance in her hair. They found a flat rock and sat. Howard cautiously put his arm around her waist and drew her closer. She rested her head on his shoulder and said, "I don't know how to say this, but I've taken a fancy to you, Yank. I have a lot of admiration for what you've done and the man you are."

"Ellen, I think I'm falling in love with you." He took her in his arms and kissed her. Ellen put her arms around him and kissed him ardently.

She laid her face against his and whispered, "I think I'm falling in love with you, too." After more kisses were exchanged, they resumed their walk.

A few days later, Rory remarked to Howard, "Looks like you and Ellen are getting pretty tight."

"I really like her," Howard said. "I think we love each other. Is that a problem?"

"No problem with me, Mate, and I know the family will approve. I'm glad you found someone. Jack has a girl, Victoria. She's a schoolteacher—lives in Dubbo with her mother. You'll meet her soon. She and Jack plan to be married."

Howard put his arm around Rory's shoulder in a silent gesture of sympathy. Rory smiled, "Don't worry about me, Mate. I've got a bloke in Warren. We're good friends. His name is Peter, and he is an artist. Paints water colors."

33

Hartford, Connecticut, April 2017

Frank continued to work at his father-in-law's company, for the two years following the deaths of his wife and baby. As the manager, he gradually took over many of Spenser's tasks, but his life was not happy.

Frank had few friends. Weekdays he lunched at the office with his father-in-law. They usually discussed company business or the current political scene. George had aged. His father-in-law's face was drawn and pale. After work, Frank returned home and looked at himself in the mirror. The face he saw reflected sorrow, with dark circles under his bleary eyes and a downturned mouth. He kept a bottle of Belvedere Polish vodka in the freezer and usually had two or three drinks before cooking a frozen dinner for himself. Frank seldom watched TV, which he found boring. Frank could not sleep in the same bed he and Susan had shared. He couldn't even sleep in the same room. He slept on a cot in the pink nursery after getting rid of the crib and the bassinette.

On a Halloween night, Frank answered the door to find a group of children with their parents chanting "Trick or Treat." Frank had nothing to give them. He could only shrug and apologize. He was depressed the rest of the evening and determined not to let another Halloween pass without rewards. The following year he was prepared, having purchased a variety of candy for the occasion. Frank left the porch light on and waited expectedly, but no children came. He was about to turn off the light when the doorbell rang. Rushing to answer, he found one little girl standing there with her mother. Frank was delighted. He proffered all the candies and tried to initiate a conversation with the child. The mother became nervous at his attention, took the child's hand and led her away. Frank watched them go, thinking of little Emily and Melissa.

Although Frank hated to dine alone, occasionally he would. This evening, he had just given his order to the waitress when a well-dressed woman got up from her table and walked over to him.

"Hello, Frank," she said. It was Cathy.

Frank started to stand. "Please don't get up, Frank. I just wanted to tell you how sorry I was to hear of the dreadful loss of your wife and baby."

"Won't you join me?" Frank asked.

"Okay," she said. She directed a waitress to bring her food over to Frank's table.

Frank was embarrassed. "I guess I should apologize. I didn't treat you decently when . . . you know . . ."

"That was a long time ago, Frank," she said.

"Anyway, I'm sorry I behaved the way I did," he told her.

"What do you do nowadays?" Cathy asked.

"I'm still working at my father-in-law's company. I'm the manager. How about you?"

"Well, I went to a community college for two years, got an Associate degree and became a paralegal. I work for a law firm here in Hartford."

"That's great. I'm impressed. Is there a man in your life?"

"No," she said with a smile, "I'm still single. What's new with Howard?"

Frank's face darkened. "We don't see each other," he told her. "I haven't seen or heard from him in years."

"How come?" she asked.

"He turned off on me. I can't blame him. After all, I tried to blame him for the drunken episode of mine in which I killed a little girl, and then he found out about you and me." Frank grew tense.

"Do you know where he is?" she asked.

"Last I knew he was working in Washington as a paramedic."

Their conversation became more relaxed and by the time they finished their dinners, the tension had disappeared. Cathy started to get up to leave.

"Let's keep in touch," Frank said.

Cathy regarded him for a moment. "O.K.," she said and gave him her phone number. She smiled and left the restaurant.

It was nice seeing Cathy tonight. I think she has forgiven me. I miss Susan, but maybe it's time to move on. I believe it's what Susan would want.

34

The following evening Frank phoned Cathy.

"How about dinner tomorrow night?" Cathy hesitated for a moment. "Maybe you don't want to go out with me? Perhaps I'm moving too fast," Frank said.

"Oh, no, I'd like to have dinner with you. I have my own apartment now," she said and gave him her address.

"How about six o'clock?" Frank said.

"Six is fine."

Frank pulled up in front of Cathy's apartment house, went in, and took the elevator to the third floor. He found her apartment and rang the bell.

Cathy greeted him. "Hi, Frank." A young child stood next to her. "This is my daughter, Rachel. Rachel, this is Mr. Frazer." The child smiled at him shyly.

"Hi, Rachel. You can call me Frank. How old are you?"

"Seven," the child said.

"Nice to meet you, Rachel. Give me five." He extended his hand, palm up, and she slapped it with a grin. Turning to Cathy, he said, "I didn't know you had a daughter."

Ignoring Frank's comment Cathy said, "Come in and sit down. We're just waiting for the babysitter."

I wonder who the father is. A previous marriage? A divorce? The doorbell interrupted his thoughts. The babysitter, a high school girl, had arrived.

"Hi, Genevieve," Cathy greeted her. "We won't be too late." Cathy turned to the child, bent and kissed her. "Have fun with Genevieve, Honey, and don't stay up too late." She and Frank left.

At the restaurant, they were seated and placed their orders. Frank ordered a bottle of wine. After the waiter poured the wine and left, Frank said, "Rachel is a lovely child. Can I ask where her father might be?"

Cathy looked at him. "Do you really want to know?"

"I do," he said.

"Well, right now, he is sitting across from me," she said.

For a moment Frank looked puzzled. He laughed nervously. "You mean . . . but I thought you . . ."

"No, I didn't have the abortion. I used the money you gave me to have Rachel."

Frank was stunned. *I'm a father! I have a little girl. A little girl like Emily, who I killed, and like Melissa, who I lost. Is God giving me another chance with Rachel?*

Cathy watched the expression on his face. "Don't worry, Frank. I don't expect you to do anything."

"But I want to do . . . something. Be a part of her life. Like being her father."

"You can see her as often as you want."

"Okay, thanks, but . . . well, tell me about her."

"She's a loving child, extremely bright. She is in 2nd grade and she can read. She has friends. She's a happy child."

"Does she miss having a father? Does she wonder or ask where her father is?"

"No, not yet."

"I don't know what to do," Frank said. "What do you think I should do? What do you want me to do?"

"I don't want you to do anything, Frank. You can do whatever you wish."

"How often can I see her?"

"Well, I work during the day, and she's in school for most of the day. So, you can see her evenings and weekends. Do you want her to know you're her father?" Cathy asked.

"Yes, I do. Certainly. How will you—we—tell her?"

"I don't think she should be told right away. Let's see how you both get along," Cathy said.

"You're probably right. I agree. She can just call me Frank."

Frank visited Cathy and Rachel almost every evening and spent weekends with them. He read stories to Rachel at bedtime and kissed her goodnight. Rachel now called him Uncle Frank and ran to hug him each time he arrived. Frank took Rachel to her soccer practice while Cathy did her errands. Afterwards, he took the child, grass-stained but happy, out for ice cream.

On a warm weekend in August, Frank took Cathy and Rachel to a lake where rowboats could be rented. Rachel had never been in a boat and was excited. She sat in the front of the boat and peered into the water while Frank rowed and her mother sat in the back. Frank rowed out into the lake as Rachel continued to gaze into the water trying to see fish. She grew animated. "I see one! There's a fish, a big one!" she shouted. Frank, facing Cathy as he rowed, did not see the child as she stood on the seat to peer into the water.

"Be careful, Sweetheart," Cathy called, but too late. Frank turned to see the little girl lose her balance and topple into the water.

"Oh, God," Cathy screamed. "She can't swim!"

Frank was horrified to see the boat move away from the struggling child. He leaped into the water, his dive moving the flat- bottom boat still further away. *I've got to reach her before she sinks.* He swam the few strokes to Rachel who started to go under. Thoughts raced through his mind. *No! Please God, not this one. Don't take this one away from me.* He reached her in seconds and brought her up to the surface.

"It's okay," he said. "Daddy's here."

He held her and turned to swim back to the boat, but a breeze moved the boat further away.

Cathy, unfamiliar with boats, screamed."What should I do?"

"Row to us!" Frank managed to call to her.

Cathy sat in the center seat, reaching for the oars, which now trailed the boat. The oars were in locks, but Cathy had never rowed a boat. Frank found it difficult to swim with all his clothes. The rowboat continued to move away from Frank and Rachel. Frank realized he must save his strength for swimming and continued to swim after the boat. Cathy was now able to use the oars to stop the boat from drifting away from Frank. He was nearly exhausted when he reached the boat, grasped it with one hand while supporting Rachel.

"Take her," he gasped. Cathy dropped the oars, knelt, and lifted Rachel into the boat. Resting for a few moments, Frank was able to haul himself into the boat and lay on the floor. Cathy cradled the crying child, trying to calm her. Frank regained his strength in a few minutes.

"Move back to the rear seat with her," he said. Frank was now able row the boat back to the dock.

Rachel stopped crying as the boat reached the dock. She was drenched and said, "You're all wet too, Uncle Frank."

An attendant helped Cathy and Rachel out of the boat. "I guess someone fell overboard," he remarked. Turning to Frank, he said, "Good thing you're a swimmer."

"You ought to provide life jackets," Frank told him. "We will never rent here again." The attendant shrugged.

Driving back to Cathy's apartment, Cathy started to undress her daughter. The child giggled with the difficulty of removing the wet dress. In the apartment, Cathy toweled Rachel off and dressed her in dry clothes. She offered a towel to Frank who removed his wet shoes.

"Sorry, I have nothing dry to offer you," she said. She produced a bathrobe for him and in the bathroom he was able to get out of his wet clothing.

"I'll throw these into the dryer," she said.

Frank and Rachel sat in the living room while Cathy produced a chocolate milkshake for her daughter.

"Thank you for saving me, Uncle Frank. Why did you call yourself 'Daddy' when you got me?" Cathy gave the milkshake to Rachel in time to hear the child's question.

Frank did not know what to say. He looked at Cathy. "I guess when I got to you, I felt like a daddy." He looked at Cathy again. "I wish I was your daddy."

"I do, too," Rachel said.

On one of the last warm days of the summer, Frank, Cathy and Rachel had a picnic at Elizabeth Park. Cathy prepared a basket with fried chicken and other favorites. They spread a blanket on the grass and after enjoying lunch, visited the rose garden. As they strolled through the garden, Rachel ran ahead, stopping now and then to smell some flowers.

Frank used the few moments alone with Cathy. "You know I enjoy being with you and Rachel," he said. "I love you both, and I want to marry you. I know Rachel likes me. We can be a happy family."

"You don't have to marry me, Frank, just because of Rachel. I like you, but I'm not sure I love you. I need some time."

"Okay, I can understand, but I'll keep asking."

Months later, on New Year's Eve, Frank came over to spend the evening with the girls. He brought a bottle of champagne and some ginger ale for Rachel. As they toasted the New Year, Frank asked Rachel, "Would you like it if your Mom and I got married?"

The little girl's face lit up, and she said, "That would be awesome. Then you could be my Daddy."

Frank turned to Cathy. "Well, how about it?"

Cathy smiled. "That was a sneak attack." She reflected on the happy times the three of them had together and realized she had come to love Frank. "I think that would be awesome." And they kissed.

Rachel jumped up and down with joy. "Now Frank, Daddy, can come to live with us."

Frank explained he had a house. "You and Mom can come to live with me."

Cathy had the master bedroom repainted and brightened. Frank and Cathy had the room that Rachel would use redecorated giving her the choice of color and décor. It was the room that he and Howard shared for many years. Frank thought of Howard. *I'd like to tell him what has happened with my life and try to make things right between us. We haven't seen each other for more than five years.*

The wedding was a small one. George Spenser was the best man. Rachel had a new dress and was the flower girl, paving the way for the bride with rose-petals. After the ceremony, the wedding party ate at a restaurant, which provided a wedding cake. Spenser took Frank aside and told him, "I'm happy for you, Frank. I'm glad you found someone. I know Susan would approve."

"Thanks, Dad."

Cathy and Rachel enjoyed living in what was now their house. They particularly enjoyed having a backyard where they could grill hamburgers during the summer months. Rachel transferred to a new school where she was now in third grade. Frank arranged for her to take swimming lessons at the Y.W.C.A. Cathy continued working at her law firm, and Frank continued as manager of the company.

A year later, Frank was saddened to learn George Spenser died in his sleep. He left everything to Frank who assumed the presidency of the company. Although the Frazer's were not wealthy, they were now "comfortable", able to take vacations, and provide for Rachel's future. For the first time in many years, Frank was content.

35

Warren, Australia November 2017

Time passed as two more crops of cotton and wheat were planted and harvested. Howard and Ellen were engaged, and Rory's prediction was accurate—the family approved.

At dinner one evening when Howard and Ellen announced their engagement, John remarked "We're happy to have you in the family, Howard. Some Yank blood could stimulate us."

Howard continued to work at the ambulance company, but spent all his free time with Ellen.

Jack brought Victoria to Warren and introduced her to the family. Vicky was shorter than Jack, only reaching to his shoulder. Nevertheless, Vicky proved to be an intense young woman, mostly serious, but with a sense of humor. She sometimes teased Jack, calling him a "big lummox" for his slow, deliberate movements. It was obvious to all that they were deeply in love.

After Jack and Vicky were married, he told his bride, "You'll like living in Warren. That's where all the culture is." Everyone laughed. Vicky's mother said. "I don't know about the culture. You do have a movie theater here. I'm sure I'll come and visit."

Jack and Vicky found a flat in Warren. Vicky rushed into the Donnelly house one evening and announced, "I got a job here in Warren. I'm going to be a teacher again." Everyone applauded.

Jack continued to work on the farm.

A few days later, Rory told the family. "My friend Peter has a flat in Warren not far from Jack and Vicky. He's invited me to move in with him. What do you think of that?" After a few moments of silence, Maureen said, "That sounds like a grand idea. That way you will be close to Jack."

On one of their late afternoon walks Ellen said to Howard, "If you still want to marry me, this would be a good time. It's spring, and the cotton has been planted. No one has much of anything to do. We could be married here on the farm. It could be a garden party."

"Sounds wonderful," Howard said. "I'm all for it."

John and Maureen sent out invitations to their friends.

It would be a civil ceremony. The local magistrate lived in Dubbo. Jack arranged for him to come to the farm and perform the ceremony.

"Don't bother to have them come to Dubbo for the license," the magistrate told him. "We can do it before the ceremony."

The weather was beautiful on the wedding day. Ellen wore a simple white dress accented with flowers. Howard borrowed a dress shirt and tie from Jack and a jacket from John. Maureen and Millie out did themselves preparing a festive spread on outdoor tables. A violinist from Warren was there to play.

The guests began to arrive at three o'clock. Seats had been arranged to provide a center isle. The ceremony was scheduled for four o'clock.

At three-thirty the magistrate arrived to be greeted by John and the happy couple. They went into the house to complete the marriage license.

"Your name, Sir?" the magistrate asked Howard.

"Howard Frazer."

"Can you provide proof of your identity?"

Howard expected this and produced his passport.

The magistrate turned to Ellen, "And your name, young lady?"

"Ellen Donnelly."

"I recall I held you when you were baptized," he said.

Ellen giggled.

The magistrate glanced at them. "I assume you are both of age, in good health, and entering into this union of your own free will?"

Howard and Ellen chorused with, "Yes, we are."

"In that case, I'm pleased to issue a marriage license. Now let's go outside. I'm dry as a bone, and I need a drink before I can perform any further official functions."

Maureen came in to inquire if they were ready.

They all walked out to the garden. John took Ellen's arm and prepared to walk her down the aisle as the fiddler played. He waited for the magistrate to refresh himself and for Howard to take his position. The fiddler, noting that the magistrate was now ready, began to play Wagner's Wedding March. John escorted Ellen down the aisle, kissed her, and handed her over to Howard.

The magistrate performed the traditional ceremony.

Jack, as Best Man, handed a ring, purchased by Rory the previous week, to Howard who placed it on Ellen's finger and kissed her. Everyone applauded and cheered.

"Thanks for the ring," Howard told Rory. "I'm embarrassed that I forgot all about it."

Rory grinned. "No problem, Mate, it was a pleasure."

The fiddler continued to play as the guests enjoyed the food and drink. The happy couple circulated among the guests, Ellen introducing her new husband to many friends.

Later, they went upstairs to Ellen's room. Howard had moved to her room that morning. Her room was somewhat larger than his, with a double bed and private bathroom.

"This is temporary," Ellen said. "Just for a while, then I want us to find a flat in town."

"That's fine. As long as we are together," he said.

The consummation of their marriage was intense, tender, and satisfying. *I love her,* he thought. *I have finally found a woman who loves me and will stay for the long haul.* They fell asleep in each other's arms.

Ellen woke during the night. They had disengaged to achieve more comfortable positions for sleep. *I really love this Yank. He's been through a lot, fighting in Iraq – trying to save his comrades. He's a hero. And then that awful Ebola. I'm so glad Rory brought him back here – to me.*

36

Warren, Australia, January 2018

Howard continued working at the ambulance company. He and Rory usually drove there together. After a few months, Ellen started looking for a flat in Warren.

On a sultry morning in January, Maureen put on a bathrobe and walked downstairs to stand in the doorway. Everyone was still sleeping. It had been a week of thunderstorms, and the air was hot and humid. She gazed over the land with a feeling of apprehension that she couldn't explain. Then she saw it, a huge, black cloud rotating rapidly and moving in her direction.

"Oh my God! It's a tornado. It's coming toward us." She shouted to wake her husband, Rory, Howard, Ellen, and Millie. "We've got to take cover. Hurry. Down in the cellar!"

Everyone rushed to the cellar in bedclothes. The power was out. In the darkness, they huddled together clutching each other.

Now the storm could be heard, a deadly hum against the background of thunder, growing louder each second. The sound was so loud they had to shout to each other to be heard. The storm struck with incredible violence, shaking the house above them.

The storm continued for some minutes, then the sound gradually began to lessen as the tornadic cell moved away. The group waited to make certain the storm was gone and then crept out of the cellar to stare at the flooded house. Heavy rain was still falling. In the dim light they looked at each other. "Where's Millie?" Maureen asked. She was the first to notice her absence. "Millie!" she kept calling. There was no answer. Everyone searched the ground floor, but Millie was not there.

Rory cautiously looked outside. After a few minutes he returned, dripping wet, tears rolling down his cheeks. "She was outside," he told them. "She's dead. She must have been trying to protect the garden. It looks like a limb from one of the trees hit her—fractured her skull. We need to bring her inside."

"She should have known better than to got outside in such a storm," John said.

"She could have come into the cellar with the rest of us," Ellen said.

"Should have, could have, doesn't matter now," Maureen said.

Howard and Rory went outside to carry Millie's body into the house. Outside, the ground was covered with golf ball-sized hail.

It was sometime before power and telephone service were restored. The family was relieved to learn that Jack and Vicky had survived. Some of the houses in Warren were destroyed leaving a number of people dead or injured.

John phoned the magistrate to report Millie's death. The family and a few friends attended her funeral. She was wrapped in a white tablecloth, her rosary in her hand. She was laid to rest in a location not far from the house, which would henceforth be the family burying ground. John read the service from the English Book of Common Prayer. When he finished, he added, "Millie always wanted children, but these were denied her. When her husband died, she adopted our family and became one of us. We came to love her and will miss her."

Jack, Rory, and Howard took turns filling in the grave. Rory played his guitar and he, Jack and Ellen sang *Nearer My God to Thee.*

Some of the mourners joined in. John announced that a suitable headstone would be obtained.

People learned the storm, a tornadic super-cell, had cut a path of death and destruction in their section of New South Wales. Twenty-four people died in Warren and the surrounding area. There were many who needed medical attention. Howard and Rory were busy working to transport casualties to the hospital. John tried to find a contractor to repair the damaged roof and broken windows. Maureen and Ellen busied themselves cleaning up the flooded downstairs.

37

August 2018

Rory noticed Howard didn't perform his tasks at the ambulance company with his usual alacrity.

"Are you O.K., Mate?" he asked Howard.

"I think so, I just feel a little sluggish. I haven't been sleeping well. I'm sure I'll be O.K." But Howard was not O.K. He was easily fatigued and lacked energy for simple activities.

"Why don't you talk to Dr. Smith?" Rory suggested.

Dr. Smith examined Howard, finding him normal except his blood pressure was too high.

"Maybe you're eating too much salt," the doctor said. "I'd like you to watch your salt intake before I give you medicine for the blood pressure."

Howard tried to avoid salty foods, but his health continued to deteriorate. Ellen told Howard his face looked puffy.

He returned to the doctor who observed swelling of Howard's hands and feet. "I get drowsy off and on during the day," Howard told him. He handed Howard an empty paper cup.

"I want a urine specimen, and I'm going to draw some blood for a few tests." Howard complied. He noticed his urine had a pink color.

The next day Smith told Howard, "You're blood urea nitrogen and creatinine are elevated, and there are red bloods cells and hemoglobin in your urine."

"What does that mean?" Howard asked.

"It indicates some form of kidney disease." The doctor took a long history from Howard. He was surprised when Howard told him of his bout with Ebola. Smith consulted his computer. "Ebola can predispose to chronic kidney disease," he told Howard. "I want you to see a kidney specialist in Sydney. I'll arrange for the referral."

Howard told Ellen what the doctor said.

"You better go to Sydney and see the specialist," she told him. "I'll go with you."

Rory drove Howard and Ellen to Dubbo, where they found a pilot who would fly the pair to Sydney. Once there, a taxicab took them to the Royal Prince Alfred Hospital where Howard was expected. He was introduced to Dr. Emmanuel Kosman, who after an examination, admitted Howard to the Renal Department. Ellen found a room in a nearby bed and breakfast.

Dr. Kosman performed a number of tests on Howard to evaluate the extent of his damaged kidneys. When these were completed, he met with Howard and Ellen. "The picture is not encouraging," he told them. "Howard's kidneys are failing, and he will soon require dialysis. He will eventually need a kidney transplant."

"How do you go about getting a kidney for him?" Ellen asked.

"Unfortunately, there are more people who need kidneys than there are kidneys available," the doctor explained. "Most kidneys come from cadavers of people who indicated they wish to be organ donors. Committees of ethicists determine priority for receiving a kidney. They consider factors such as Australian citizenship, military service, and the age of the recipient. Some people die while waiting for a kidney, so Howard might have a long wait. The other possibility," Dr. Kosman continued, "is a kidney donated from a close family member. Then, of course, the transplant could be done immediately. The other advantage of a family donor is the reduced likelihood that the kidney will be rejected."

"How is it possible for someone to donate a kidney? Wouldn't donating a kidney be risky?" Ellen asked.

"People can function fine with only one kidney," the doctor explained.

"Suppose my body rejects the donated kidney? What happens then?"

"We will then have to treat you by suppressing your immunity with drugs." The doctor left, leaving Howard and Ellen depressed.

"Maybe we should just let me go," Howard said.

"Nothing doing!" Ellen told him. "I haven't had enough time to enjoy you as a husband, and besides, I want us to have a few kids. Raise a family. We'll figure something out."

38

Hartford, Connecticut, August 2018, 4:00 AM

The phone rang early in the morning.

"It's four a.m.," Cathy said. "Who could be calling at this hour?"

"Would you please answer it?" Frank said.

Cathy said, "Hello?"

"Is Frank Frazer there? Can I speak to him?" the caller asked.

"Who is this?"

"My name is Ellen Frazer. I'm calling from Sydney, Australia. My husband is Howard Frazer, Frank's brother. Howard is very sick."

"Could you please hold for a minute?" Cathy said. "Wake up, Frank. There's a woman calling from Australia. She says she's Howard's wife, and he's very sick. I think you'd better speak to her."

Frank took the phone. "I'm Frank Frazer," he said. "Can I help you?"

"Are you Howard's brother?" Ellen asked.

"Yes, I am. What's the problem?"

"Howard is quite ill," Ellen said. "He needs a kidney, preferably from a close relative. If he doesn't get a kidney, he will die."

"Why a close relative?"

"Kidney's have to match," Ellen tried to explain. "Otherwise, the body rejects them. Would you be willing to come to Australia to be tested?"

"What do you mean tested?"

"Tested to see if your kidney would match. If it does, would you be willing to donate one of your kidneys?"

"Don't I need both of my kidneys?" Frank asked.

"No, a person can do just fine with one kidney," Ellen told him.

"Can I speak to Howard?"

"He's in the hospital," Ellen said. "Perhaps I should tell you that he doesn't know I'm calling you."

"Can I call you back? Please give me your phone number," Frank said. "I'll get back to you," and hung up.

He turned to Cathy, "She wants me to go to Australia to see if I can donate a kidney to Howard. She said if he doesn't get a kidney he'll die."

Cathy was silent for a few moments. "I think you should consider going to help him, Frank. He's your brother."

Many thoughts came to Frank's mind. *I remember how Howard protected me when we were kids. How close we were. I remember trying to blame him for my drunken episode killing little Emily, and I remember getting Cathy pregnant and demanding she have an abortion. There would have been no Rachel.*

"I have to help him," Frank said. "He's my brother."

"You're right," Cathy said. "You've got to go. She—Ellen, expects you to call back and tell her if you'll be coming."

Frank dialed Australia. "Ellen? It's Frank. I'm coming."

"I was hoping you would," Ellen said. "Call me with your flight plans, and I'll meet you at the airport in Sydney. Please come soon."

Sydney, Australia, September 2018

Frank cleared customs and entered a large area filled with people coming and going. He walked toward the exit until his eyes fell on a woman displaying a large placard reading "Frazer." He approached her.

"Ellen?" he asked.

She smiled and extended her hand noting that Frank was taller and slimmer than Howard, but the Frazer resemblance could not be missed.

"Welcome to Australia, Frank. How was the trip?"

"Long," Frank told her, "but I'm glad to be here. How is Howard doing?"

Ellen's face darkened. "Not too well. His kidneys are failing, and he already had to be dialyzed. I'll take you to see him." They found a taxi and started for the hospital.

"Everybody's driving on the wrong side of the road," Frank remarked.

"Only this is the right side, Yank," the taxi driver called back, and they both laughed.

When Ellen entered his room, Howard was sitting in a chair wearing a bathrobe and pajamas. "There's someone here to see you," she announced as Frank walked into the room. For a few moments the brothers stared at each other in silence.

"Frank!" Howard said. "What are you doing here?"

Frank walked over to where Howard was sitting, and the brothers shook hands. "I thought you might like a visitor, so I just dropped by," Frank quipped. *He looks older, as if he has been through a lot,* Frank observed.

"How did you . . ."

"Ellen called me," Frank said.

"It's been a long time, Frank," Howard said, not knowing what else to say. "What have you been doing with yourself?"

"There's a lot to tell," Frank said. "I guess you know I was in prison. When I got out, my former boss was nice enough to give me my job back. And then, this sounds funny; I met and married the boss' daughter. Her name was Susan. We were happy together."

Happy after what you did to Cathy? Howard thought. "Was, were? What happened?"

Frank's face had a sad expression, and his voice fell. "She was pregnant, and she and the baby girl both died in childbirth."

"Jesus Christ, that's terrible. I'm sorry, Frank," Howard said.

Frank continued, "After a few miserable years, I ran into Cathy again. She had a child, Rachel. My daughter. Thank God she never had the abortion. We eventually married. Rachel is now eight, and I love them both dearly. So what have you been doing?" Frank asked.

I am glad Frank and Cathy are happy together. Can I forgive him for the things he did? After all, he didn't rape her. She must have consented. And I didn't own her. And as far as Frank trying to blame me for the accident, he must have been scared shitless when the cops came. He's my brother, and I have carried these feelings far too long. And now he has come all the way to Australia. Of course I forgive him.

"I guess you remember I enlisted in the army—trained as a combat medic. My unit deployed to Iraq where I was wounded."

Ellen broke in, "Howard was awarded the Purple Heart and the Bronze Star medals. He's a hero."

"Oh, Ellen," Howard said embarrassed. "Anyway, after I was discharged, I joined Doctors Without Borders. I went to Liberia in West Africa to help fight Ebola. I even came down with it—damn near died. While I was there I met Rory Donnelly, Ellen's brother, who convinced me to come home with him to Australia. He has a wonderful family, including his beautiful sister, Ellen. They have a big farm where they grow cotton and wheat. Ellen and I fell in love. We've only been married a few months, and now my damn kidneys are kicking up."

"That's one of the reasons I came to see you," Frank told him.

"What do you mean?"

"Just maybe, I can lend you one of mine."

Howard was shocked. "You mean to tell me you're going to let them take out one of your kidneys and give it to me? Why?"

At this point, Dr. Kosman entered the room. Ellen introduced Frank to him. "Doctor Kosman, could you please explain the possible advantage of using Frank's kidney?"

The doctor turned to Howard. "Most of the kidneys we transplant come from donors unrelated to the recipient. The recipient's body regards the donated kidney as foreign and his immune system begins to reject the kidney. So we have to treat the recipient with powerful drugs, which suppress his immune system to prevent rejection. Otherwise, the kidney would fail. These immunosuppressive drugs have unwanted side effects. But if we can find a donor closely related to the recipient there is a good possibility the kidney would not be seen as foreign and therefore not be rejected . . ."

"And that's where I come in," Frank said.

"Of course," the doctor explained. "We have to do some tests to check compatibility."

"I don't know what to say, Frank," Howard said.

"Don't say anything. Let's see what the tests will show."

39

September 2018

The tests showed significant histocompatibility between Frank and Howard. The doctor asked Frank to sign a document confirming he was voluntarily donating one of his kidneys to Howard without any pressure or promise of reward.

Frank signed without hesitation. He placed a phone call to Cathy. "I'm going to do it," he told her. "It's his only chance, otherwise he will die."

"I understand," Cathy told him. "I know how you must feel. I'll keep my fingers crossed."

"How are you and Rachel?"

"We're both fine. We miss you."

"I miss you, too."

The surgery was scheduled for the following morning. The procedures would be performed in adjoining operating rooms. The night before the surgery, Frank entered Howard's room, "Are you ready for the operation?" Frank asked.

"How can you do it?" Howard asked him. "They're going to take out one of your kidneys, leaving you with only one. Suppose something happened to that kidney—you'd be in deep shit. I can't let you go through with this."

"Look Howard, you're my brother, and I want to do it. Besides, one kidney is all you need to function."

A nurse entered and beckoned to Frank. "We need you now, Mr. Frazer."

Frank walked over to Howard and shook his hand. "Good luck, brother." Then, without warning, Frank bent and kissed him on the forehead before leaving with the nurse.

In the evening, the brothers were prepared for surgery. Further food was withheld, their bodies were washed and each was given a mild sedative.

In the morning, they were given further sedation, moved to gurneys, and wheeled to operating rooms. The procedures took several hours. Afterward, still asleep, they were transferred to a dimly lit recovery room, near to each other under the careful observation of a nurse who monitored their vital functions.

Frank was the first to waken, still groggy, and asked the nurse, "How's he doing?"

"He's doing fine," the nurse said and offered him sips of water.

Howard awoke and called over to Frank, "How are you doing, Bro?"

"Fine," Frank said.

Eventually, they were discharged from the recovery room and wheeled to Howard's room where Ellen waited. A bed for Frank had been installed.

Ellen walked over to Howard and kissed him. "How do you feel?"

Howard managed a grin. "I'm okay."

She walked over to Frank where he lay and spoke with him.

The results were encouraging the following day. Howard's new kidney began to function. A technician came in daily to draw a blood sample from Howard's vein.

"Why do I need more blood tests?" Howard asked her.

"We are checking your creatinine level to see how your kidney is functioning. Creatinine is a waste product the kidneys remove from the blood."

The brothers were both on pain medication. Over the next few days, their dressings were inspected, and they were allowed regular meals.

"This is like when we shared a room as kids," Frank said.

They spent hours recounting the past years.

Frank asked, "What was Iraq like?"

"Not too bad when you are bivouacked away from rebel areas, but you always had to be alert for an attack. The battles were small but hellish." After more discussion Howard asked, "What did you do when you got out of prison?"

"I got a job with an IT company. The president, George Spenser, was a terrific guy. He became a surrogate father to me."

"I'm sorry about Susan and the baby, Frank. It must have been tough."

"Yeah, the world came to an end for me. George forced me to go back to work. He was a kind man. When he died, he left everything, including the business, to me. Then I found Cathy and Rachel." Frank sighed and was silent for a few moments. "Tell me about the Ebola."

"It was the worst thing I ever experienced, much worse than Iraq. We had hundreds of cases everyday and not enough beds or medicines until Obama sent troops in to help. All in all, there were about 5,600 cases in Liberia alone. More than half of them died."

October 2018

Ellen visited every day. After a few weeks, their sutures were removed, the dressings changed, and they were able to walk around.

Frank talked about returning home. Ellen prepared to take Howard back to Warren when he awoke one morning feeling feverish. His temperature was 102°, and he had pain around the incision. Howard felt dizzy and was nauseated. His hands and legs became swollen, which were signs of fluid retention.

Dr. Kosman came in and told Howard, "These are indications your body is trying to reject the new kidney. Your immune system recognizes the kidney is foreign and is attempting to get rid of it. We must give you medicine to stop the rejection. We will suppress your immune system with a polyclonal antibody."

Over the next few days, Howard worsened. His urine output decreased, and he gained several pounds due to fluid retention. He became depressed. "I hoped the transplant would work," he told Ellen.

40

Ellen did not want to show her distress to Howard, but she cornered the doctor. "What do you think is happening?"

"It's too early to tell," he told her. "Right now, I would say the chances of his recovery are fifty-fifty."

Frank cancelled his return flight. He called Cathy, "Howard started to reject my kidney. I'm going to stay here for a while. I'll keep in touch."

The following morning Dr. Kosman came in accompanied by another doctor whom he introduced to Howard. "This is Doctor Gupta. He is a psychologist. He has just returned from a year in the U.S. at UCLA where he studied MBCT."

Howard greeted Dr. Gupta. "What is that?" Howard asked.

Dr. Gupta smiled. "It's a new method of treatment called Mindfulness-Based Cognitive Therapy."

"Do I need psychotherapy?" Howard asked.

"Many of our organ transplant rejection cases have benefited from it. We'd like you to try it," Dr. Kosman said.

"I don't want to be hypnotized," Howard said.

"Not to worry," Dr. Gupta told him.

Howard hesitated. "Okay. I'll give it a try."

"Please come with me," Dr. Gupta said.

Howard accompanied the psychologist to a small room containing what appeared to be a comfortable seat and an ordinary chair. A high window provided daylight, but otherwise the illumination was subdued.

Dr. Gupta gestured for Howard to take the seat. He found it to be relaxing.

Dr. Gupta explained, "A simple two minute exercise will help you understand Mindfulness far better than I can. Would you like to try it now?"

"Sure."

"Sit comfortably with your back straight but relaxed," Dr. Gupta said. "Take a few deep breaths. Breathe normally. Notice the sensations of the breath as it moves in and out of your chest and belly." Dr. Gupta was silent for a few minutes as Howard followed the instructions.

Dr. Gupta continued in a quiet voice, "As thoughts arise in your mind, simply acknowledge them and then bring your awareness back to the breath. Notice the sensations of the air as it enters your chest. Notice the sensations of the chest and belly as the muscles expand and contract. Notice the sensation of cool at the edge of the nostrils on the in breath, and the warmer sensations on the out breath."

Dr. Gupta was silent for several minutes. Then he continued quietly, "Each time you notice yourself getting lost in thought simply bring awareness back to the breath. This attention to awareness, by concentrating on breathing, is the key to this training."

Howard found he was mostly able to concentrate on his breathing. Occasionally thoughts of his kidney, Ellen, Frank, and Dr. Kosman arose, but Howard soon got the knack of coming back to the breath. He found it very soothing. After what seemed to be a long time, but was only five minutes, Howard heard the faint sound of a bell ringing.

"Well done, Mister Frazer," Dr. Gupta told him. "That's all for today."

Back in his room, "How did it go?" Frank asked.

"All I did was breathe. I don't know how it's going to help, but I'll give it a try."

The next day, Dr. Gupta appeared and led Howard to the same room. Howard sat in the seat and waited.

"Today I would like to invite you to do what's called a 'body-scan'. I'll guide you through it. Let's get started," Gupta said.

Howard heard a single faint chime of the bell.

"Bring your awareness to your left foot. Notice the sensations of temperature, pressure, moisture, and how it feels. Like yesterday, as thoughts come into your mind, notice them, but bring awareness back to the body. Notice the sensation in the toes and heel. Now bring your awareness into the ankle." Howard tried to comply and became aware of the feelings in his left foot.

After a minute, Dr. Gupta continued, "Now, bring your awareness to your left calf, the shin, the knee, and the back of the calf."

Howard noticed a tingling in his calf.

In this manner, Dr. Gupta was able to guide Howard in visualizing each and every part of his body. By the time the bell struck three times, marking the end of the session, about thirty minutes had passed.

"Just what is the purpose of these exercises?" Howard asked the psychologist.

"They are helping you to stay present with your experience without judging, and teaching you to let your thoughts, worries, and emotional reactions come and go. This is the 'Being' mode. In the 'Being' mode, we are only thinking of ourselves in the present. Most of the time, we are in the 'Doing' mode, with thoughts of the past, present, and future."

"How did it go today?" Frank asked when Howard returned.

"Good. It's interesting. I'm getting ready to learn how to meditate."

During the next few days, Howard's condition worsened. He produced less urine than the amount of water and other fluids he drank, and his creatinine level remained high.

Dr. Gupta continued working with Howard every day. In a few days, Howard found he was able to meditate for as long as twenty minutes. Although Howard was on pain medication, he could still feel the pain of his incision during these periods. He was able to stay present with each sensation for a while before dire thoughts and "what ifs" arose.

"See if you can feel the sensations in your new kidney," Dr. Gupta suggested while Howard meditated. "You might want to welcome it and encourage it to function." Howard did not laugh. He tried to concentrate only on his breathing and his new kidney.

After several days, Howard produced more urine. His temperature returned to normal, and he gradually eliminated the excess fluid his body had retained. He no longer required pain medication. After another week, he felt much better, and the doctor told Ellen, "His creatinine level has come down to normal. I believe we have stopped the rejection."

Seven days later, Howard and Frank were discharged from the hospital. Howard would continue to require immunosuppressive drugs for an indeterminate time.

Ellen insisted Frank spend a weekend in Warren before returning home. Back in Warren, the Donnellys were glad to see Howard. They greeted Frank warmly. Ellen showed Frank around the farm and introduced him to her brothers, when they appeared.

Frank spent the weekend with Howard and the Donnellys, but he was anxious to return home. After saying goodbye to the family, Jack drove Frank, Howard and Ellen to Dubbo where an air taxi waited.

En route, Ellen asked Frank, "I guess you'll be glad to get home?"

"Yeah," he said. "I miss Cathy and Rachel."

"Let's plan on seeing each other again," Howard said.

"I hope to bring Cathy and Rachel to Australia for a visit," Frank said.

"And I would like to show Ellen the U.S. when we visit."

At the airstrip, Howard walked Frank to the small aircraft. The brothers embraced. Howard took Frank by the shoulders. "There's something I need to tell you, Frank. I understand why, under pressure, you tried to blame someone else—anyone else for what happened, and you thought of me. I shouldn't have let that become such a big deal. I forgot about it long ago and what happened between you and Cathy . . ."

"What happened between Cathy and me when we first met was at a party. We both had a lot to drink. When she became pregnant I treated her badly and told her to have an abortion. Thank God, she didn't. It was more than six years before we met again."

"Those things happen," Howard said. "I was never in love with Cathy or she with me. We were just high school kids. Anyway, what I want to say is, I love you, Frank."

Tears appeared in Frank's eyes. The men embraced.

"And by the way, thanks for the kidney," Howard said.

"Anytime, Bro," he smiled and entered the aircraft.

Howard walked back to the truck, watched the airplane taxi, take off and disappear in the distance. *It took a lot for Frank to leave Cathy and Rachel and come all the way to Australia to give me one of his kidneys. His kidney makes it possible for me to have a life with Ellen.*

41

January 2019

Howard continued to receive immunosuppressant medication. His strength returned, and he was able to go back to work. Every few weeks, he and Ellen received letters from Rachel, addressing them as "Uncle Howard" and "Aunt Ellen." These letters inquired into Howard's health and expressed her wish of someday visiting Australia.

"It must be great to have a child," Howard said to Ellen one evening. "I envy Frank and Cathy having Rachel."

"Yes, it must be fun to watch a child grow, her first steps, first words, progress in kindergarten, school, and graduation," Ellen said.

Howard chuckled. "We could have a son, you know, " he said, and they both laughed.

Ellen continued looking for a flat in Warren. The tornado had destroyed or damaged many houses, and as yet no flats were available.

Ellen decided to go back and take another course at the college, but after several months, she experienced episodes of nausea throughout the day. "I don't think it's anything I ate, and I'm not feverish," she told Howard.

"Why don't you stop in and see Dr. Smith?" Howard suggested.

The nausea continued, and Ellen phoned the doctor for an appointment. When she returned to the farm Howard asked her, "What did the doctor say?"

Ellen smiled at him. "You don't have to envy Frank and Cathy anymore, Uncle Howard. You've just been promoted a notch. You're going to be a father. Rachel will have a cousin."

Howard was jubilant. *I'm going to be a father! We're going to have a baby. Maybe a girl or even a boy. A son.* "I'm so happy. I know you've been wanting a child," he said.

On Sunday, the whole family came over for dinner. Rory brought Peter. After dinner they all gathered around the spinet. Maureen played old songs that everyone knew accompanied by Rory on his guitar. From time to time, someone called for a favorite song. As the evening deepened, Rory said, "Let's do *Danny Boy."* It was a popular sentimental song of an Irish mother lamenting her son's departure.

Ellen sang the melody with her clear voice, Rory and Jack harmonizing as everyone hummed the tune. As the song ended, Ellen looked at Howard with a smile and simulated a kiss.

Howard gazed with affection at the family gathered around the spinet. Tears filled his eyes, and his heart swelled with happiness.

They were his family now. *This is my home.*

AUTHOR'S NOTE

The information about Ebola including outbreaks and epidemics is true.

All persons and characters in this book are fictitious with the exception of President Obama, President Ellen Johnson Sirleaf, Alan Alda, Georgia O'Keeffe and Grandma Moses. Any similarity to persons living or dead is coincidental.

P.D.E.

ACKNOWLEDGEMENTS

Andria O'Neil helped with research and the preparation of the manuscript. Samantha Lovetere assisted with copyediting and research. Diane Myers, Paula Myers and Lenore Mand all provided helpful comments after reading the first draft. Toby Stein, a professional editor, provided a detailed critique that was insightful and instructive. The U.S. Army unit in Beaufort, S.C. helped with information on current military training. Attorney Robert Sparrow provided legal information and Steven E. Lurie, Ph.D. told me about Mindful Based Cognitive Therapy. Art work by Tovero and Marks.

Finally, my wife Connie gave unstintingly of her time almost every day. Without her help, this book would not have been possible.

Other books by the author:

Stranger In Time
And Evil Shall Come
Marika
INCIDENT IN GENEVA: Human Survivors in the Distant Future

Non-Fiction:

Understanding Infectious Disease
The Biomedical Scientist As Expert Witness

CPSIA information can be obtained
at www.ICGtesting.com
Printed in the USA
FSOW01n1803090417
32862FS

9 781634 921763